something

A Horatio Wilkes Mystery

rotten

ALAN GRATZ

speak

An Imprint of Penguin Group (USA) Inc.

SPEAK

Published by the Penguin Group

Penguin Group (USA) Inc., 345 Hudson Street, New York, New York 10014, U.S.A.

Penguin Group (Canada), 90 Eglinton Avenue East, Suite 700, Toronto, Ontario, Canada M4P 2Y3
(a division of Pearson Penguin Canada Inc.)

Penguin Books Ltd, 80 Strand, London WC2R 0RL, England

Penguin Ireland, 25 St Stephen's Green, Dublin 2, Ireland (a division of Penguin Books Ltd)

Penguin Group (Australia), 250 Camberwell Road, Camberwell, Victoria 3124, Australia
(a division of Pearson Australia Group Pty Ltd)

Penguin Books India Pvt Ltd, 11 Community Centre, Panchsheel Park, New Delhi - 110 017, India

Penguin Group (NZ), 67 Apollo Drive, Rosedale, North Shore 0632, New Zealand
(a division of Pearson New Zealand Ltd)

Penguin Books (South Africa) (Pty) Ltd, 24 Sturdee Avenue,
Rosebank, Johannesburg 2196, South Africa

Registered Offices: Penguin Books Ltd, 80 Strand, London WC2R 0RL, England

First published in the United States of America by Dial Books,
a member of Penguin Group (USA) Inc., 2007
Published by Speak, an imprint of Penguin Group (USA) Inc., 2009

1 3 5 7 9 10 8 6 4 2

THE LIBRARY OF CONGRESS HAS CATALOGED THE DIAL EDITION AS FOLLOWS:
Gratz, Alan, date.
Something rotten: a Horatio Wilkes mystery / Alan Gratz.
p. cm.
Summary: In a contemporary story based on Shakespeare's play Hamlet, Horatio Wilkes seeks to
solve the murder of his friend Hamilton Prince's father in Denmark, Tennessee.
ISBN 978-0-8037-3216-2 (hc)
[1. Family problems—Fiction. 2. Murder—Fiction. 3. Water—Pollution—Fiction.
4. Pollution—Fiction. 5. Mystery and detective stories. 6. Tennessee—Fiction.]
I. Title. PZ7.G77224Som 2007 [Fic]—dc22 2006038484

Speak ISBN 978-0-14-241297-8

Designed by Jasmin Rubero
Text set in Century Old Style

Printed in the United States of America

A secret suspicion

Hamilton put a hand to the screen, but the image had already cut to black.

"I wouldn't believe it if I hadn't seen it," I said.

Hamilton turned. "I believe it. And I know exactly who did it."

"Who?"

"My uncle Claude."

Frank and Bernard shuffled around, trying very hard to be somewhere else and not succeeding.

"You don't know that," I told him.

"Dad practically said as much! He said his name!"

"That's just who interrupted him, that doesn't mean—"

"He took over the company when Dad died," said Hamilton. "And the bastard married my mother." Hamilton spoke through his teeth. "He married *my mother*."

Sometimes I get stubborn, and this was one of those times. "Look, Hamilton, I don't know what this thing is between you and your uncle, but you can't just go jumping to conclusions. You can't be *sure* it was him."

Hamilton stepped away and wouldn't look me in the face.

"No. No, I guess you're right. We don't know *for sure*," he said, mocking my cautiousness. "But until we do, not one of us can breathe a word about this. To anyone."

OTHER BOOKS YOU MAY ENJOY

To my middle school and high school
English teachers:

Tom Pettitt, John Tatgenhorst, Martha Gill,
Dale Norton, Warren Heiser, Neil McMahon,
and Mary Jo Potts—see? I was listening.

Special thanks to Liz Waniewski for drinking the water, Regina Castillo for letting me steal her joke, Jon Manchip White for teaching me the art of murder, Brian Winfrey for listening to me talk about Horatio for years, William Shakespeare and Raymond Chandler for their invaluable assistance, Wendi and Jo for their infinite patience and support, and teachers of English everywhere.

**"Something is rotten
in the state of Denmark"**

-HAMLET, Act 1, Scene IV

CHAPTER ONE

—☠—

Denmark, Tennessee, stank. Bad. Like dead fish fricasseed in sewer water. I said as much to my friend Hamilton Prince as we rode in his 4x4.

"You get used to it," he told me. "Just think of it as the smell of money."

And here I had always thought money would smell better.

The Elsinore Paper Plant was the source of the stink, and the money behind the Prince family fortune. Elsinore makes the paper that you use in your printer, the paper you read the sports scores on, and the paper you wipe yourself with. They make just about every kind of paper there is except the kind money is printed on, but enough of that comes rolling back in that they don't have to bother. It was also the first place Hamilton wanted to take me when I arrived in Denmark for my month-long summer visit. I wasn't real excited to go watch paper being made, but Hamilton was looking for any excuse to get out of the house and I didn't say no.

I nodded at an open beer in the cup holder. "One for the road?"

"It's just one, and we're not going far." He nodded over his shoulder. "Root beer for you in the cooler."

We hadn't talked since I had called a week ago to see if my visit was still on, but Hamilton was quiet and I let him stew. He had a lot going on, what with his dad dead and his uncle marrying his mom and all. I wanted to ask about everything, but I didn't want to push it.

A light drizzle kicked up outside, and Hamilton threw on the wipers as we turned down a little access road. A sign told me we were headed toward the Elsinore Paper Plant, but my nose could have told me just as well. The main complex was far enough away from Hamilton's house that you couldn't see it, but not far enough away that you couldn't smell it. Maybe it was once, but not now. The paper plant had been owned and operated by Hamilton's family for generations. His dad was CEO when he died, and now his uncle Claude ran the company. Someday Hamilton would run it too. I thought it must be nice to have a six-figure salary waiting, and I said so.

"I hate it," said Hamilton. "It's like a prison. My own personal prison."

Hamilton's always been a little on the melodramatic side. It was a song and dance I'd heard before and I'd never believed it, but the tone of his voice this time gave me second thoughts.

At first I thought it was a trick of the foggy windshield, but as we drove up to the security gate outside the plant I saw a girl standing by the road holding a sign. Her hair was flat from the rain and her face was smudged from wiping away the drizzle, but you could still tell she was gorgeous. Her Windbreaker broke in all the right places and her jeans hugged her in ways they don't teach you in kindergarten. Hamilton pulled up beside her and ran the window down.

"What are you *doing*?" he asked her.

"Protesting." She stuck her sign in his face. It said: "Elsinore Paper Poisons the Copenhagen River."

"Give me a break," Hamilton said.

"Denmark's been giving you guys a break for a hundred years. It's time for Elsinore to come clean. That river is so polluted, it would kill you to drink it." The rain was coming a little harder now, but the girl was undaunted.

"Nobody's going to see you here," Hamilton told her.

She held her sign over her head to block the rain. "*You* saw me," she said.

I liked this girl already. "Hey," I called to her. I pulled off my dad's old St. Louis ball cap and tossed it through the open window at her. She caught it with her free hand and didn't let it fall into the mud, which I appreciated.

The girl pulled her hair back into a ponytail and slipped on the hat, and I saw I was wrong. She wasn't gorgeous; she was stunning.

Her head now covered, the girl brought her sign back down in Hamilton's face. He shot me a nasty look and gunned the 4x4 on through the plant gates.

"You don't have to encourage her," he said.

"Friend of yours?" I asked.

"Her name's Olivia. She's a townie."

I glared at Hamilton, but he ignored me. We both went to an expensive private boarding school called Wittenberg Academy in Knoxville, Tennessee, and when you reduced the school to its lowest common denominators you got two groups—the boarders and the townies. I'm a townie. I'm *from* Knoxville. I go to school at Wittenberg, but I don't live in the dorms like the rest of the students. There are twenty-three of us townies. We know one another, and everybody knows us. It costs us less to go to Wittenberg—much less—and if it didn't, most of us couldn't afford to go. Sometimes the rich kids won't have anything to do with us, but Hamilton had never been like that. That's why I didn't like the way he called Olivia a townie, like she was beneath him or something. It wasn't like Hamilton, and it pissed me off.

"You mean the Olivia you used to write letters to and call every other night on the dorm phone?" I asked him.

"Yeah," he said. He kept his eyes on the driveway. "I kind of stopped calling. I think she might be mad."

"You think?"

Hamilton shot me another look, but I dodged it. I have to admit, I was a little sore. Part of it was the townie thing, and part of it was the way Hamilton just dropped girls, like there were always more waiting in line. Worse, there always *was* someone waiting. Hamilton's got that sort of blond Nordic swimmer's build girls dig. Good chin, hard nose. Dresses sharp. He's well-read, well-bred, and well-heeled. Everybody loves him. Everybody but his ex-girlfriends.

But I'd been friends with Hamilton long enough not to be a player hater. He was the kind of guy who could have easily looked down his nose at somebody like me, but he didn't. We'd bonded on the baseball field our freshman year, and I'd been Hamilton's unofficial third roommate ever since, using his room as my base of operations while I was on campus.

Hamilton parked the car. "Come on, we have to check in at the security station." He grabbed his beer and dashed through the rain to a small concrete building. I took a deep breath and reminded myself (again) that Hamilton wasn't himself right now, and I left my root beer and my attitude in the car and followed him.

Inside, one of the security guards was practically hugging Hamilton.

"Why haven't you come to see us since you got back?" the guard asked him. The patch sewn on his rent-a-cop uniform said *Bernard* in cursive.

Hamilton shrugged. "You know. Busy."

Bernard nodded sympathetically.

"We was real sorry to hear about your dad. He was good people," the other guard said. His patch said his name was Frank.

"Not like that uncle of yours," Bernard mumbled. Frank elbowed him.

"Say what you want, guys. You're among friends," Hamilton told them. "Speaking of, this is my best friend from school. His name's Horatio Wilkes."

We shook hands. From the looks on their faces, Hamilton's introduction was all it took to earn me their lifelong devotion.

"Should we tell him?" Bernard asked.

Thunder rumbled outside. It fit with the sudden chill in the air.

"Tell me what?" Hamilton asked.

Frank looked around, as though there might be spies in the little ten-by-ten-foot room we were in. He beckoned us into the monitor room, where a dozen screens flickered with security camera images of the Elsinore Paper Plant and Hamilton's home. One of them showed the front gate where Olivia still stood, holding her protest sign and wearing my baseball cap and looking pretty.

Bernard pulled an old coffee tin off a high shelf and withdrew an unlabeled videocassette. "We prob'ly should've shown you this as soon as you got back from school," he said, "but like you said, there was other stuff going on."

"You guys got Olivia on tape half-naked or something?"

Hamilton joked, trying to break the strange tension in the room.

Frank gave Hamilton a weak smile and started to say something, but then just popped the tape in the cassette player instead.

The central monitor in the bank of screens flickered with static, then adjusted itself. It became an image of the inside of the plant. A huge machine thrummed in the background, rolling acres of paper onto huge reels. The digital time stamp at the bottom gave the date as more than two months ago.

"This is thrilling," Hamilton said. "It's almost as exciting as—"

Hamilton's father walked into the picture.

"—watching paint . . . dry," Hamilton finished. He sat down and stared. It had to be a shock. The last time Hamilton saw his father alive was during Christmas break. He hadn't talked to his father for two months after that, and then one day the headmaster pulled him out of English and told him his dad was dead.

The weird thing was, this didn't look anything like Hamilton's father. The last time I had seen him he was middle-aged, with sandy brown hair and a smooth complexion. The man on the screen had snow white hair and a face like a walnut. He looked like he was a hundred years old, but it was Mr. Prince, sure enough. There was a sad, hollow look in his eyes that I knew but couldn't place.

Hamilton turned to look at me, and then I knew where I'd seen it before.

"Hamilton," his father said, startling all of us, even the guards.

"Dad? What happened to your face? Your hair?" Hamilton said to the ghost in the machine. For some reason it didn't seem crazy for him to be talking to a videotape.

"Hamilton, if the boys show you this tape, it means something bad has happened. Something very bad. It means I've been murdered."

Frank and Bernard seemed to shrink away, and Hamilton and I were alone with the ghost of his father.

"It was poison," his father said. "Slowly, over the course of weeks. Maybe months." He coughed hard. "I should have told you, I know, but I didn't want you to worry. Same with your mother. I—I saw all kinds of doctors. Got treatment. I thought I was going to get better." He coughed again. It was worse this time, and I could see Hamilton wince.

Hamilton's dad's eyes drooped. "Never knew how the stuff was getting into my system. But now, now I think somebody *did* this to me. On purpose." He hacked again, spitting up little bits of phlegm and blood. "I can't prove anything, but—"

Off camera, a door banged closed. Hamilton's father looked over his shoulder, then whispered quickly into the camera.

"It was all because of the paper plant." He broke off, coughing again. "You think you know someone. You trust them, and then—"

A shadow fell across his face. Someone stood near Hamilton's father, still off camera.

"Hello, Claude," Hamilton's father said. "Taking more dioxin samples? I, uh, there was something wrong with this security camera. Just checking it out." He looked back at the camera. "I'm sure if my son was here, he could fix it."

Hamilton put a hand to the screen, but the image had already cut to black.

"I wouldn't believe it if I hadn't seen it," I said.

Hamilton turned. "I believe it. And I know exactly who did it."

"Who?"

"My uncle Claude."

Frank and Bernard shuffled around, trying very hard to be somewhere else and not succeeding.

"You don't know that," I told him.

"Dad practically said as much! He said his name!"

"That's just who interrupted him, that doesn't mean—"

"He took over the company when Dad died," said Hamilton. "And the bastard married my mother." Hamilton spoke through his teeth. "He married *my mother*."

Sometimes I get stubborn, and this was one of those times. "Look, Hamilton, I don't know what this thing is between you and your uncle, but you can't just go jumping to conclusions. You can't be *sure* it was him."

Hamilton stepped away and wouldn't look me in the face.

"No. No, I guess you're right. We don't know *for sure*," he said, mocking my cautiousness. "But until we do, not one of us can breathe a word about this. To anyone."

Frank and Bernard inched out from among the filing cabinets and nodded.

"Why not?" I asked.

"It's family business," Hamilton told me. "Princes don't air their dirty laundry."

"Are you crazy? We need to go to the police with this."

"No. Not a word. To *anyone*. Swear."

"We swear, Mr. Prince," Frank and Bernard said, almost in unison.

Hamilton fixed me with a stare. *"Swear."*

Right then and there, I made a mistake. If I hadn't, I might have saved us a lot of trouble. Maybe even kept somebody from getting shot. But nobody ever accused me of being a genius.

"All right already. I swear." I felt like a third grader sealing a deal with a spit-shake.

"You may not be sure in your head, Horatio, but I know for sure *here*," Hamilton said. He pointed to his heart.

On a monitor behind him, I saw Olivia holding her poster at the gate. I could still read the words: "Elsinore Paper Poisons the Copenhagen River."

One thing was for sure. Something was rotten in Denmark, Tennessee, and it wasn't just the stink from the paper plant.

CHAPTER TWO

— 💀 —

A servant met us in the driveway with a couple of open umbrellas so we wouldn't get wet from the rain. He didn't have one for himself, and I noticed he got drenched in the process. When we were safely inside he told us we had just missed dinner, which I suspected was the real reason behind the timing of our little excursion.

The smell from the plant wasn't any better here in the house, and I began to wonder if I was going to have to burn all my clothes when I went home at the end of the summer. I gave my shirtsleeve a sniff and didn't like what I came away with.

Hamilton led me up a flight of carpeted stairs to the second floor of his house. Of course, when I say "house," I'm using the term loosely. Mansion would be more like it. Or maybe castle. I knew the Princes were rich, but until it was staring me in the face I didn't realize they were *super-villain* rich. The place didn't smell like money, but it sure looked like it.

"My room's down that way. My mom and . . . her new husband, their room is around the corner down the west wing."

That last bit was delivered with a withering gaze down the

hall at his mom's room. I just thought I should report that, in the interest of journalistic integrity or whatever.

"Anybody ever get lost in this place?" I asked.

"Everybody that lives here is lost," said Hamilton.

Again with the melodrama. But then, considering what we'd just heard on the security monitor, maybe Hamilton wasn't overplaying it after all. See, Hamilton's dad died two months ago, and his mother, Trudy, went and got married again before they could even clean out her dead husband's closet. But she didn't just get married—she married her husband's brother. That was weird and all, but Hamilton acted like it was more than that. Like his mother had betrayed the family somehow. And now with his father's appearance on *Prime Crime Live,* I could see that anger turning into something harder. More cruel.

All of which made things kind of awkward for me. To be fair, my summer visit was scheduled before Hamilton's dad died, and *long* before Mrs. Prince's wedding plans. Then again, lots of things take longer than his mother's remarriage. Like toast. Besides, it's kind of crappy to back out on your best friend just because his family has suddenly become the Wikipedia entry for *dysfunctional*.

Hamilton Prince and I had known each other since freshman year. Most kids at Wittenberg come from other places close by: North Carolina, Georgia, Kentucky, Ohio. There are loads of international students too: a bunch of Saudis, some Eastern Bloc refugees, and this Belgian kid everybody calls "Belgium" because we can't pronounce his name. And then there are the people like Hamilton who come from little Podunk Tennessee towns to escape the schools where they still tear the evolution pages from textbooks.

Hamilton's particular little hickville is Denmark, Tennessee, and let me tell you, it's pretty rough. Just driving through, I can already tell you that a big night in Denmark is cruising the Sonic Drive-Thru and getting drunk in the parking lot of the Piggly Wiggly.

"Come on," said Hamilton. "Let me show you the home theater my dad put in for me before he—"

He started to choke up, and I interrupted him. "Look, Hamilton, this is wrong. I don't have to be here. I've got six sisters back in Knoxville who can't wait to start running my life again."

"No, Horatio, I like that you're here. You're like the one sane person in my life right now."

We shared one of those weird guy moments where one of us reveals his weak, vulnerable side and neither of us knows quite how to handle it. So we did what we always do: Pretend it didn't happen.

"Let me show you this big screen," Hamilton said. "You gotta see the PlayStation on it."

"Lead on," I told him.

When Hamilton said "home theater," he really meant it. It was like a real movie theater inside his house. There were five or six rows of theater seats, the cushioned kind that fold up when you stand, and the screen was bigger than some of the multiplex screens I've seen.

"We got tired of driving an hour to the nearest movie theater," he explained.

"Well, I hate driving fifteen minutes to Starbucks, but you don't see me building a coffee shop in my bedroom," I joked.

"We've got video, DVD, even a real film projector. PS3, Xbox, there's a popcorn machine back here, and down here . . ." Hamilton opened a cabinet, revealing a stash of liquor bottles. "Voila! There's even root beer for Mr. Boring."

"Yeah," I said. "Because you're a barrel of laughs when you get drunk."

Hamilton flipped me a root beer, and made himself a whisky on the rocks. He took a swig and shook his head. "If you had a life like mine, you'd drink too."

I looked around at Hamilton's home theater. I was tempted to tell him if I had a life like this I wouldn't have much to complain about, but his dad just told us he was murdered, so I shut it.

"Don't worry," Hamilton said. "We'll make a drinker out of you yet."

I popped the top on my root beer. "Better men than you have tried."

We stood there for a minute, drinking in silence. There was a lot to talk about, and none of it had to do with root beer or video games and we knew it. I decided it wouldn't be me who brought it up.

"So I should probably get my stuff out of my car," I said.

"The help should have done that already," said Hamilton. "Let's go figure out where they put you."

The house was full of big, empty rooms. I mean, they had stuff in them—beds, chairs, bureaus—but you could tell nobody lived in them. The really weird thing was that each of them had some sort of theme: *Wizard of Oz,* medieval, Victorian, dogs.

"After my dad died, my mom went kind of crazy redecorating the place," Hamilton explained. "She did every room differently." He flicked the light on in the next one.

"There's my bag," I said. It was sitting on a huge four-poster bed framed by big, sweeping green velvet curtains. The rest of the furniture looked antique—a big cherry wardrobe, a little rolltop desk, leather-covered, high-backed chairs. Pictures of Rhett Butler and Scarlett O'Hara stared daringly across the room at each other from the ornate wallpapered walls.

"Oh, not the *Gone with the Wind* room," Hamilton moaned. "Come on, get your stuff. We'll put you somewhere else."

I grabbed my bag, but it was empty.

"They put my clothes away?" I asked.

"All part of the service," said Hamilton. He opened a drawer and pulled out a stack of my T-shirts.

"Don't. Leave it," I told him. "It's fine. It's not like I'm going to be hanging out in here, with that entertainment room down the hall."

"They must have put you here so you'd be close to my room. It won't be any trouble—"

"Frankly, Hamilton, I don't give a damn." I swooned on the big feather bed. In a room like this, there was no other way to put it. "At least it's not the room with all the Barbie dolls."

"Suit yourself," Hamilton said. He sat in one of the big leather chairs. He swirled the drink in his glass, and we were suddenly back to the uncomfortable silence. This time he decided to start.

"They're reading the will tomorrow," he said. Hamilton stared at his ice cubes. "Want to go with me?"

"And here I was afraid no one was going to ask me to the will reading, after I had a dress picked out and everything."

"So you'll go?"

I sat up. "Hamilton, I don't belong there. This is family business. I'm happy enough to spend the morning killing zombies and throwing touchdowns on your big screen."

"Come on, Horatio, I need your help here. You heard my father. Somebody killed him. Maybe Claude."

"Maybe not."

"Whatever. But I need to know who and why."

I got up and put my bag away in the bottom of the wardrobe.

"What makes you think my guess is better than anyone else's?"

"You're like the smartest guy I know."

Great. So now somebody *was* accusing me of being a genius.

"You're the one who got an A in philosophy," I told him.

"And you got A's in everything else," Hamilton said. "Please, Horatio. You gotta help me solve this mystery."

I sat in a chair with a flower-print skirt on it.

"It's not a mystery," I told him, "it's a problem. Somebody killed your dad. The problem is figuring out who did it. A *mystery* is why there's anything worth killing another person for to begin with. I can help solve your problem, but I'm no good at mysteries. I'll leave those to you."

"Fair enough," Hamilton said. He stood and offered me his hand. For the second time that day, I found myself shaking on something I had no business agreeing to.

Hamilton clapped me on the shoulder. "Come on, let's go kill us some zombies." He left the room. At the risk of getting lost without my guide, I stayed behind a few seconds longer, wondering if I wouldn't have been better off vegging on my couch and watching *Columbo* reruns all summer. I sighed. I had given Hamilton my word now, *twice,* and there was nothing to do but go through with it.

I looked around the room and caught Scarlett's picture again. She reminded me in her wonderful Southern drawl that tomorrow was another day.

But that's exactly what I was afraid of.

CHAPTER THREE

—💀—

I needed one of those big plastic color-coded directories they put in malls to find my way around the house the next morning, but I got lucky and found the escalator downstairs. From there on out I was as lost as Theseus in the labyrinth until I heard voices coming from a room down a hall. The six-inch-thick carpeting let me walk up quiet as a sigh and I bent my ear around the door for a listen.

"I don't understand," said an older man. "Are you saying Olivia and Hamilton—have some kind of relationship?"

"Oh, for God's sake, Dad." A younger male's voice, late high school, maybe college-aged. "You can't seriously tell me you didn't notice."

"It's none of your business!" came a hushed but angry voice. It was the girl who had steamed up my window from the other side of the car last night. I leaned against the wall just outside the entrance, not ready to interrupt.

"It *is* our business. Tell her, Dad."

"Well, it certainly . . . that is, there might possibly be compli— Have you been on actual dates?"

"Oh sure. If *Larry* was seeing someone, you'd have already

had her over to the house to eat dinner and pick out china patterns."

"Don't turn this into 'Nobody ever notices me.' You're avoiding the question."

"Is this how they teach you to handle hostile witnesses at law school? Am I being cross-examined?"

"I'm not *in* law school yet. I'm pre-law." He sighed, frustrated. "Tell her, Dad. Tell her Hamilton's no good for her."

"Oh. Well." His voice lowered. We were in Hamilton's *house* after all. "He's a fine enough boy, I suppose, but as the only son of our employer—I mean, our ex-employer—by which I mean the only stepson of our *current* employer—"

"He's using you, Liv," Larry cut in. "You see that, don't you? When he goes back to that snotty prep school in Knoxville, you think he's really going to carry a torch for you? When he's got a dozen rich little hotties fawning all over him? You're good enough for a summer fling, but you're not marriage material for a Prince."

I know there's this rule that family can say all kinds of nasty things to each other that they'd never let a stranger get away with, but Larry was way over the line and I didn't have to be in the same room to know it. I gave a super-fake stage cough and stepped inside, sending the old man to the ceiling. Sure enough, Olivia had tears in her eyes. She turned away quick hoping I wouldn't see. Larry and Pops were oblivious, so I gave her a minute to collect herself while I played the fool.

"Oh, sorry," I told the boys. "I was looking for the food court."

"The, er, the what?" the old man asked.

I nodded vaguely over my shoulder at the rest of the house. "I took a left at the Toys R Us, but I got lost somewhere around the Pier One."

"We're kind of in the middle of something," said the one who had to be Larry. He was about four inches taller than me, and looked to have already put on the freshman fifteen guys get when they go off to college and suddenly get thick. I pegged him as twenty/twenty-one. When you grow up the youngest of seven children, you get an eye for ages and stages.

"So I heard," I told him. "I'm Horatio Wilkes, a friend of Hamilton's from Wittenberg."

I threw Wittenberg out there on purpose, just to make Larry worry I might have heard him bad-mouthing Hamilton and his snotty school. I thought about mentioning our rich little hotties too, but it was more fun to see him sweat.

"Horatio?" the dad said, testing the name and offering a hand. It's a weird name, I know—but chicks seem to dig it.

Pops seemed harmless enough, so I gave him the old nod and firm handshake. He was older than I would have thought for someone with kids in high school and college, but maybe it was the balding white hair and the tiny round squinters he wore that made him look ready for the old folks' home. Other-wise his grip was strong, and he was pretty spry for an old dude.

"Paul Mendelsohn, private solicitor for Elsinore Paper International and the Prince family. This is my son, Lawrence, and my daughter, Olivia."

"We've met," Olivia said, all cleaned up now. She was wearing my St. Louis hat, a simple tank top, and those hip-hugging jeans.

There were awkward smiles all around. I shoved my hands in my pockets and rocked back and forth on the balls of my feet. Larry cleared his throat.

"I guess I better be getting back to school," he said.

"Summer school?" I asked. "You flunk something?"

Larry turned red. "Of course not. I'm taking summer semester so I can graduate early and start law school in two years. Some of us can't *afford* the ten-year program."

"It's good that you're hurrying," I told him. "I hear there's a lawyer shortage."

Mendelsohn Jr. frowned, trying to figure out if he should sock me or ignore me. He settled on the latter, which meant he wasn't as stupid as he looked.

"If you need any more help, Dad, just let me know." Larry turned to his sister. "And *you* remember what I said, Olivia. I'm just looking out for you. I don't want to see you get hurt."

"Then maybe you shouldn't come home so often," she said, taking the words right out of my mouth. Larry shook his head and left while Pops looked around for something to do with his wringing hands.

"I still think we should discuss this," Olivia's father said. She didn't have a smart remark for him, but she didn't look happy about it. I stayed where I was, the big white elephant in the room they couldn't talk around. Finally Paul relented, sparing me a mirthless smile. "Well. There will be time enough for talking later, I suppose. At present, I must go and prepare for the reading of the will. I'll see you at home."

The Princes' private solicitor bid me adieu with a nod, and Olivia relaxed like her drill sergeant had just left the room. She glanced at me, and her eyes told me she saw my save for what it was. From the looks of it, she was both appreciative and embarrassed.

"Thanks for the hat," she said. She gave the bill a tug. It had that stained, faded look from being washed about a hundred times, but where it should still have been pretty soaked, it was dry. She'd shown my cap some love and run it through the dryer.

"You looked like you were about to drown out there," I told her.

She crossed her arms and leaned back against a table. "I think there are a few people who wouldn't mind if I did. So, your name's Horatio? What, did your mom lose a bet?"

See? Always a hit with the ladies.

"You live in Denmark?" I asked her.

"Born and raised. Not that I won't be on the first bus out of here when I graduate."

"Can't take the smell?"

"Among other things," she said.

"So, you seem pretty fired up over this environmental thing."

"Shouldn't I be?"

"I don't know. I don't know how bad it is. Beyond the smell, I mean."

"It's bad, all right. Worse than the smell. The smell, you get used to."

"Yeah," I said. "People keep telling me that."

"You should see for yourself. The Copenhagen is a dead river now."

"Maybe I'll hike down there one day then and see. Pay my respects."

I caught her giving me the once-over. I was wearing my usual summer uniform—worn-out white T-shirt, khaki pants, black Converse high-tops. My dirt brown hair could probably have used a comb this morning, and what little stubble I had was due for my weekly shave. My last girlfriend called me scruffy-looking, but that was right before she kissed me.

"You and Hamilton been friends for long?" she asked me.

"Since freshman year," I told her. "Baseball team."

"Oh, right," she said, touching the hat. She wasn't offering to give it back, and she had to notice I wasn't asking for it. The great thing about loaners is you always know you're going to hook up later to collect.

"He ever talk about me?" she asked.

This was tricky territory. "Used to," I said.

"So what was it—a rich little hottie?" she said. I knew what she was asking: why Hamilton dumped her.

"No," I told her. "Hamilton's usually the love-'em and leave-'em type, but with you it was different. I think I actually caught him writing you a poem once."

She blushed softly, but her sadness overcame it. "So what happened?" she asked.

I had to think about that one. "First it was his dad," I told her. "You can't imagine how hard that hit him. It was like somebody pulled his plug. He walked around like a zombie for weeks. He didn't even talk much to the people he saw every day."

Olivia nodded. She could forgive him that, I could see. But we both knew there was more.

"Then Trudy and Claude happened. Do you have any idea why he would hate his uncle so much?"

She gave that some thought and shook her head. "No. I mean, he's just as much of a jerk as Hamilton's dad. Neither one of them gave a damn about what they were doing to Denmark."

"Well, for what it's worth, he hasn't had anything to do with *any* girl since he broke up with you," I told her.

Olivia wasn't any happier to know this. I think she might have rathered it *was* another girl. At least that way there'd be someone to hate besides Hamilton. Which meant she wasn't ready to let him go, no matter how much she acted otherwise.

As if on cue, Hamilton strolled in. Olivia stood like she'd been caught making out with me, then just as quickly leaned back all casual. Hamilton missed it, but I didn't.

"What are you doing here?" he demanded.

"Just looking for a jackass," she told him. "Oh look. One just walked in." She turned and gave me a smile. "See you around, Horatio."

Hamilton refused to watch her as she slid by, but my eyes never left her. I don't figure to be thinking about marriage for another fifty or sixty years, but I was definitely interested in Olivia for more than a summer fling.

"You horning in now?" Hamilton asked.

"What if I was? I thought you two were through."

"Come on," he said. "The will reading's getting ready to start."

I noticed he didn't answer my question.

CHAPTER FOUR

—💀—

The office where they were reading the will looked like a page from *Field & Stream* magazine. A rainbow trout hung on a plaque over the fireplace, twisting in ecstasy like he couldn't be happier he'd just been hooked. Beneath my feet, a large black bear lay plastered to the floor as though a sixteen-ton weight had flattened everything but his head, and boy was he pissed.

"Impressive, isn't it?" said a thick, bearded man I took to be Hamilton's uncle Claude. "Took him down myself."

"With your bare hands?" I asked.

Claude laughed like that was the funniest thing he'd ever heard. Hamilton found a corner to sulk in, so Claude did his own introductions.

"You must be Hamilton's friend Horatio. Family name?"

"Yeah. We're all named Horatio, me and my six sisters."

Again with the laugh. He was trying way too hard. He nodded to the blond woman sitting at a small meeting table. "You know Hamilton's mother, Trudy, don't you?"

Mrs. Prince was one of those moms you know is attractive but you try not to think about it too much. She's not a supermodel or anything, but she's definitely the kind of soccer mom the ref takes a second look at. The few times we'd met she'd been really nice to me, like she appreciated that Hamilton found somebody to hang with who isn't a Neanderthal. Despite swapping husbands faster than Superman changes clothes in a phone booth, she was all right in my book.

"We've met," I said. I gave her a nod and a sympathetic smile. "I'm sorry for your loss."

For a split second, she looked confused. I guess I was a little late with the condolences.

"He means Dad," Hamilton snapped. "You remember him, don't you? Your first husband?"

Mrs. Prince looked at her lap, and I felt like a dolt for feeding the fire.

"Hamilton! Apologize to your mother," Claude demanded.

"Her first."

Claude didn't have a bit of control over Hamilton, and they both knew it. My friend crossed his arms defiantly and leaned back against a wall, and I debated using one of my patented non sequiturs to lighten the mood. I decided it wouldn't help, and planted my hands in my pockets instead.

"Horatio, we've got a bit of business to take care of here today," Claude told me. "Maybe you could wait upstairs. Watch a movie."

"He's here because I asked him," Hamilton said, daring Claude to say no.

His uncle sighed. "Well, in that case, would you care for something to eat?" He motioned to a tray of glazed things on the table.

"Got any fruit?" I asked.

"Fruit?"

"Yeah. You know—small, round, lots of pretty colors. You've seen pictures."

Claude couldn't figure out if I was just being funny or giving him crap on purpose, but either way he didn't like it. It was like someone took an eraser and wiped the fake smile from his face. What was underneath was the coldest, meanest mug I had ever seen outside that movie about the serial killer who ate his victims. My skin prickled, and I began to understand why Hamilton hated this guy.

I shrugged and snared a Danish. "Oh well," I said. "When in Denmark."

Claude's face didn't revert to faux-amused. He eyed me like I was a new player on *Who's My Enemy?* which was fine by me.

The Prince family solicitor, Paul Mendelsohn, bustled in like some kind of cartoon character. I half expected Bugs Bunny to pop out of his briefcase and send papers flying while Paul juggled his glasses.

"Sorry I'm late, everyone. I seemed to have left the will in some papers I had filed, er, in my car."

Paul took a seat at the table. Claude joined him, pulling up a chair close to Mrs. Prince. She leaned into him. They would have looked like almost anybody's idea of a happy couple except for that tricky business with the dead brother/husband. Hamilton shared a ferocious look with the bear on the floor and stayed where he was. Caught in limboland, I figured what the hell and took a seat at the table. Claude sent me a disapproving frown, but I passed it right back.

"Yes. Let's see. Let's see." Solicitor Paul fumbled through his briefcase and extracted a weighty document printed on pages as long as my arm and signed in triplicate. "Oh. I, well, I didn't think to make copies for everyone to follow along with."

"That's all right, Paul," said Claude. The happy face was back, and the quick change was creepy. "Nobody here speaks legalese anyway. Why don't you just hit the high points?"

Paul cleared his throat and straightened his glasses. "Yes. Very good. Let's see . . . high points. High points . . ."

He squinted at the tiny print on the will, flipping forward and then back again as though he had perhaps missed something he should have found. I began to think I really *would* have been better off upstairs watching a movie. My eyes wandered to a shelf full of trophies and plaques on the wall above us. They were all Claude's, but the joke was they were all second-place finishes and honorary memberships in local fraternal orders and civic clubs.

"Ah yes. Here we are. 'I, Hamilton Prince the Fourth, known to my friends and family as Rex, being of sound mind and body, etcetera, etcetera . . . do hereby bequeath to my beloved wife, Trudy, all my legal possessions, including the family home in Denmark, Tennessee, the beach house on Hilton Head, the cabin in Aspen, the private jet, and of course Elsinore Paper International and all its subsidiaries . . .'"

I zoned as Mendelsohn rattled off the company holdings. Everybody called Hamilton Sr. Rex because things kind of get confusing when every firstborn boy is named Hamilton. And people make fun of *my* name.

Mendelsohn descended into "etceteras" and asked if he should continue.

"No, thank you, Paul," Mrs. Prince said. "But tell me, does my marriage to Claude give him any ownership of Elsinore Paper whatsoever?"

"Er, um, well, no. The will names only yourself as inheritor. Legally speaking, all of Mr. Prince's possessions—er, the *late* Mr. Prince's possessions—belong to you and you only."

"Would you draw up papers then, please, making Claude half owner of everything with me?"

The request was like an atomic bomb in the room. Alarms went off in my head. I could practically feel the radiation coming from Hamilton from three yards away.

"Um, well, yes," Paul stammered. "If you're sure. That is, if that's what you want to do."

I studied Mrs. Prince, seeing her in the new light of a nuclear blast. Was she just a crazy, love-struck fool, or was there more going on here? Could half the estate be some kind of reward to Claude for disposing of Rex Prince? Did he have something on her, like nude photos she made when she was in college and needed the money? Did he hypnotize her somehow? Did she have amnesia? Had I read too many cheap crime novels?

"I'm sure," Mrs. Prince said. She looked right at Hamilton as if making a point. "Claude is my husband now. We share everything."

"You should think of me like a second father, Hamilton," Claude said.

Hamilton exploded. "A second father!? I liked the first one just fine!"

"So! Hey!" I said, standing. "Hamilton. How about that tour of the dungeon now, huh?" We so did *not* need to go where this conversation was going.

"There is one more order of business," Paul said. He shuffled through papers as though he was oblivious to the shouting match happening around him. "It is my legal duty to inform you now as the, ahem, soon-to-be *co*-owners of Elsinore Paper International, that there has been an official takeover bid from Branff Communications."

"Branff?" I said, trying it out. It was as silly on my lips as the lawyer's.

Claude slammed a fist on the table and made us all jump. "We won't sell!"

I frowned. If Claude was behind Rex Prince's death, a corporate buyout would be perfect. He could liquidate the plant, earn enough Benjamins to wallpaper the moon, and never do another day's work in his life. So why was he so hot *not* to sell?

Paul cleared his throat and cleaned his glasses with his tie.

"Technically speaking, the board of trustees must hear the bid and make a decision, but as . . . part owners, you should hold considerable sway on the vote. I believe Mr. Branff will be here tomorrow to present his offer in person."

"So sell it," Hamilton said. "Who wants to live in this stinking place anyway?"

"Our family built this plant, Hamilton. I would think that would mean something to you."

"This plant was a penny-ante operation until Dad took over and you know it," Hamilton told his uncle.

Only Mrs. Prince hadn't responded. Her eyes said she was somewhere—or some time—else.

"Wait a minute," Claude said. I saw a lightbulb flicker over his head and he turned to his wife. "Didn't you date some guy named Branff back in college, Tru?"

Mrs. Prince returned from wherever she was. I guessed she had been revisiting a particular row of frat houses on memory lane.

"Yes. Ford. Ford Branff. He's the head of Branff Communications now. I dated him right before I met Rex. We remained very good friends."

"What a surprise," Hamilton said. "Yet another man my mother has shacked up with wants to take over the plant. Do you think he'll want to be a second father to me too?"

I cursed myself. All the talk of selling the plant had made me forget to get Hamilton out of here and now I was too late. Tears sprang from Mrs. Prince's eyes. She left the room in one direction, and Hamilton bolted away in the other. I stood at the table where Claude and Paul still sat, feeling like I'd just been pantsed in front of gym class.

The three of us shared a moment where we all wished we were somewhere else.

"So," I said, "Scrabble, anyone?"

CHAPTER FIVE

— 💀 —

No one took me up on my offer of a friendly board game, so I joined Hamilton upstairs, where he was already fixing himself another drink. This time he kept the bottle. I pulled a root beer out of the mini-fridge.

"A little hard on your mother back there, don't you think?"

"Damn it, Horatio, they used the flowers from my father's funeral to decorate the wedding reception. You want me to take it *easy*?"

I settled into one of the big comfy chairs and waited for the show while Hamilton poured himself another.

"Why don't you drink it straight from the bottle?" I asked him. "Better yet, maybe we could set you up with an IV."

"Shut up."

I drank my root beer, which amounted to the same thing.

"Women are all the same, you know that?" Hamilton asked. The ice in his glass rattled, and he gave them more company. "They're weak."

Hamilton was given to making blanket statements. Mrs. Prince's decisions were difficult to understand, I granted him that, but I had a hard time indicting an entire gender. Especially one I was more than partial to.

"Care to make any sweeping gestures about mothers too?" I offered.

He elaborated on that theme with some choice—and technically accurate—profanity.

"Okay," I said. "I get that your mom remarried very quickly. And yeah, it's kind of weird that she married her dead husband's brother."

Hamilton spared me a glance that thanked me for stating the obvious. I got to my point.

"But what's with the hostility? Ever since they got married you've been mad at every woman and couple and uncle out there, regardless of race, creed, color, or national origin."

"Just one uncle," Hamilton said.

"Yeah. But you were hating on the guy *before* you thought he killed your dad."

"It's worse than that, Horatio. He's a parasite." Hamilton leaned forward, and it all poured out. "You don't know him the way I know him. For *years* I watched my dad support Claude through every one of his ridiculous ideas. The real estate seminars, the dot-coms, the alpaca farms. He always came to Dad for money for his schemes, and Dad always gave it to him."

"And I'm guessing none of them worked."

"Not just because they were stupid. Because Claude could never finish anything. Dad always said that Claude was a smart guy, that if he'd just stick with it, see something through to the end, Claude could be rich. But that's not Claude. He wants instant gratification. Dad never saw that, but I did. He could never have done what my father did. He couldn't have spent thirty years building Elsinore into an international powerhouse. Claude just wanted to get rich quick. The firstborn in every generation of Princes inherits the paper plant, and Claude missed out. Now, by marrying my mom, he's found a way in. Convenient, huh?" Hamilton sat back.

Maybe not convenient enough. Patiently poisoning somebody over weeks and months didn't equal "getting rich quick" in my book. It also didn't seem to fit Claude's MO, but I didn't share that with Hamilton.

"Okay, I see why you're not a member of the Claude Prince fan club. So why hate your mother?"

"Because she was too stupid to see him for what he really is: an ingrate and a fool and a leech. And now . . . "

And now a murderer. That's what he was thinking. He wasn't in the mood to argue it with me again, or maybe the thought suddenly sobered him. Either way, he figured he held the answer in his hands and drained his glass again. He was putting the booze away so easily, I had to wonder if he'd gotten a head start before the will reading.

"A little early, isn't it?" I asked.

Hamilton answered me with another drink. He was well on his way to a place I had never been and didn't want to go.

It's not for religious reasons or moral outrage or anything that I don't drink. When we go to ball games, my dad has a beer or two, and he's pleasant enough. But the first time I ever went to a townie party where people were drinking, I watched a girl I cared about get blasted on shots and then get pawed by half the guys in the room. Later that night she turned blue, and I wrapped her in blankets and kept the puke wiped off her face even though she couldn't remember my name.

That was the first and last time I ever had a drink.

I've been to plenty of parties and keggers since then, though. People know the root beers in the fridge are mine, and they mostly let me be. Every so often, you get somebody who can't be happy unless everybody in the room is drinking, and he'll try something stupid like pouring vodka in my root beer when I'm not looking. Guys like that pass out soon enough, though, and for the rest of the night, the girls who keep it under control are mine to chat up.

"She's always been the kind of person who needed people around," Hamilton said quietly. "My mom, I mean. She can't go anywhere alone. Has to be talking on the phone, or have a friend over. When Dad died, I know she must have been lonely . . . but marry *Claude*? I mean, couldn't she just have gotten a dog?"

Thus began the melancholy portion of our program. I've dealt with a lot of drunk kids in my day, and can classify most of them one of three ways: silly drunks, sleepy drunks, and sad drunks. Hamilton was definitely in that last camp.

"Hamilton," I said. I waited for him to find me. "Hamilton, do you really want me to figure out what happened to your father?"

"What's the point? What difference would it make?"

That was the alcohol talking. I figured I had a pretty small window where he'd be uninhibited but still coherent, and I needed answers if I was going to help.

"How did your dad die, Hamilton?"

"What?"

"Your dad. How did he die exactly? What did they tell you?"

"One morning he just didn't wake up. My mother woke up in bed beside him, and he was already dead. She—she called Claude before she called the security guards."

"Why?"

Hamilton shrugged and swirled the drink in his tumbler.

"I guess she needed a warm body to take his place in bed."

I considered this new information while Hamilton downed another gulp. If Claude and Mrs. Prince were close—maybe even lovers—she might have called him over to help cover something up. If she was innocent, it could very well be that she just couldn't deal with waking up next to her dead husband and turned to the only person she could think of to help. It would certainly freak *me* out.

"What did he die of, exactly?"

"Cancer. That's what Claude told Mom, at least. He took care of everything."

I sat back. Cancer was deadly, but hardly a murder weapon. You couldn't just give somebody cancer, could you? Not without handing them a big chunk of Kryptonite or something.

"Didn't your father say he'd been poisoned?" I asked. "In the videotape?"

"Yeah. Dad said he was poisoned. *Claude* says he died of cancer. Who do you believe? I mean, did you see dad's *face*? You could hardly recognize him! Cancer doesn't do that."

I had no idea what cancer could do. Was Rex's cancer really just a cover story? Hamilton was ready to send Claude up the Copenhagen River, and I was beginning to wonder if Mrs. Prince shouldn't sail with him. I didn't know enough yet to be sure, and the only way I *would* know would be to get my hands on an autopsy report. Somehow I doubted that was going to happen.

"Your uncle came to your dad for money, but were they friends?" I asked.

Hamilton shrugged. "They were brothers."

"But did they really like each other? Did they hate each other's guts? Did they wear matching suits for Easter? You've got to give me something more."

"Claude was the younger brother, and my dad took care of him, okay? I mean, they drank together and went hunting together sometimes, but it's not like they were best friends or anything. Claude was always jealous over the plant and my dad resented his begging, but that didn't stop the handouts. And when my dad wasn't giving him money, he was setting Claude up with jobs around the plant to help him get by."

I stood and paced in front of the big movie screen. Hamilton was slipping into that place where moving his mouth to speak was just too much to bother with, but I wanted to get more out of him while I could.

"What jobs? What did Claude do at the paper plant?"

"I don't know. Everything. Truck driver, mechanic, salesman, foreman."

"Chemist too?"

"Yeah." He paused. "Wait, how did you know?"

"From the video. Your father asked him if he was taking more dioxin samples."

"Oh. Hey. That's good." Hamilton closed his eyes and rested his chin on his chest.

"Sort of a jack-of-all-trades, then?" I prompted him.

Hamilton's head lolled back. "Jack of *no* trades, more like it. Never did anything very long."

"How about Claude and your mom?"

Hamilton blinked. "What?"

"Claude and Mrs. Prince. Were they close?"

"What the fu—" Hamilton started to arrange himself to get up. "What is that supposed to mean?"

"You wanted me to get to the bottom of this, remember? That means things might get pretty ugly. You sure you can handle that?"

Hamilton stood and swayed. His hands knotted into fists. "What are you suggesting about my mother?"

And there it was again. Like Larry cutting Olivia to the quick, Hamilton could call his mom a slut in front of a room full of people, but the minute somebody else hinted she might have had an affair with her husband's brother, it was pistols at thirty paces.

"I'm not suggesting anything. I'm asking you point-blank if she was sleeping with Claude."

I got the e-mail that Hamilton was going to take a swing at me long before the fist came by snail mail, and all I had to do was step out of the way. It helped that he was already drunk off his ass. His punch whiffed empty air, and I gave him a little push that sent him sprawling over the comfy chair where I had been sitting. I stepped back and got my knuckles ready for a scrape, but Hamilton started making an odd, strangled sound, and I relaxed. He was snoring.

I put his half-empty bottle away and threw a blanket over him, adding another category to my list: the angry drunk. Silly drunks break furniture. Sleepy drunks break wind. Sad drunks break hearts. But angry drunks are the worst of all. They end up breaking noses.

Or worse.

CHAPTER SIX

—☠—

Hanging out with a sleeping drunk is about as much fun as watching somebody vacuum, so I headed outside instead. The sun was shining, white clouds dotted the high blue sky, and the scent of pine might almost have been noticeable if the wind hadn't been blowing the nose-clogging stench of the paper plant toward the house.

A shiny black Land Rover drove up and parked at the bottom of the concrete steps that led to the front door. I expected a herd of servants to come running, but nobody showed. Instead, a smartly dressed Hispanic guy climbed out of the driver's side and crunched gravel as he strutted around the front end of the SUV. He wore a fitted cowboy shirt, black leather pants, and boots that had once been the skin of something that slithered. There was even a red bandana tied around his neck. He looked like he'd just stepped out of a Broadway musical.

The gaucho stopped in front of me and looked up the stairs like I wasn't there. I looked around to see what he was staring at, but we were the only two people there. When I glanced back, he was sizing me up with a hand on his hip and a pinched face like something stank worse than the paper plant.

"Your mother dress you?" he asked.

That was particularly rich, coming from a guy dressed like Howdy Doody. I gave him a defensive smile.

"If you're looking for the rodeo," I told him, "I think it's already left town."

The tip of the gaucho's tongue slipped out between his lips and he touched the end of his little finger to it like there was something tasty there, but his eyes weren't smiling. I buried my hands in my pockets, and we stood there daring each other to blink until I heard the front door open and shut behind me, followed by the click of high heels on the steps.

Mrs. Prince interrupted our little showdown. "Hello, Horatio." She turned to the gaucho. "Thank you, Candy."

The gaucho shifted his attitude to Mrs. Prince, and suddenly he was all smiles. "*De nada,* Miss Trudy." He pulled the car key out of his pocket and handed it over.

I blinked. Candy the Cowboy was part of the help.

Mrs. Prince looked for something in her purse and Candy left me with a cold look as he sidled by. I turned and watched him go up the steps and into the house, suddenly not comfortable turning my back on him.

I've visited friends before who have servants, and it's always a very strange thing to me. I try to hang up my own coat or get my own car, but they won't let me. Like it's against the rules. I always wonder what life is like for someone whose job it is to wait on people hand and foot. What part of yourself do you have to be able to put away not to dump a drink in the lap of the lady of the house when she's testy? Or maybe they don't put it away at all. Maybe they turn it into something cold and hard, something that gnaws at them the rest of their days.

Mrs. Prince had found whatever she was looking for, and when I looked back she was waiting to talk to me. She was dressed differently from when I had seen her at the will reading. Now she had on a slim, light-colored pantsuit with a tight blouse that definitely flattered her, and once again I tried to remind myself that this was my best friend's mother.

"I'm sorry about that business earlier," she said.

I guessed she was talking about the will reading. "Me too," I told her. "I shouldn't have been there. But Hamilton . . ."

"Yes," she said. "Hamilton."

The few times I had seen them together before the second wedding, Hamilton and his mother had gotten along famously. They were so alike, after all—both blond-haired, blue-eyed, card-carrying members of the Beautiful People Club. Life is easier for the beautiful people, and don't let any sad-sack guidance counselor convince you otherwise. And it's doubly easy for beautiful people with piles of cash. Quadruple easy.

"Heading into town?" I asked.

"Elsinore sponsors the local community theater," she told me, her attempted smile still radiant. "I'm not quite feeling in the mood for it, but I promised I'd help get things ready for opening night."

"Really? What's the play?"

"It's—um . . ." She blushed. "To tell you the truth, I can't remember. I think it's based on some Shakespeare play. Being sponsors was all Rex's idea. He loved the theater. When he died—when he died I sort of stepped in, you know? For him more than anything. He would have wanted it that way."

I hated when people said that. Nobody knows what anybody really wants when they're alive, so what makes us think we know them any better when they're dead?

I nodded anyway, wondering at the strange vibe I was getting from her. She was sad about Hamilton's dad, or at least it was still an awkward topic. That meant she was human. But there was something else there, like she wished she didn't even have to talk about it. That could be the dread over having to go into town and suffer through two dozen renditions of "I'm so sorry about your husband," or it could be something else. I wished I had been able to get a straight answer out of Hamilton about his mom and Claude, but that wasn't likely to ever happen.

"Would you like to go with me?" Mrs. Prince asked. Go with her? I felt blood rush to my head. Was Hamilton's mom really inviting me to go somewhere with her? Alone?

"A friend was going to come with me, but she had to back out," she said. "And I've barely convinced Claude to come to opening night, let alone get him down to the theater to help."

What was I getting all hot under the collar for? I was being stupid.

"No, really. Thanks. I just came outside for a walk."

Mrs. Prince gestured at the car. "You sure? I'd love the company."

One of my early teenage fantasies played itself out in my head as I imagined Mrs. Prince's offer meaning something more, and I had to shake myself out of it. *Get a grip, Horatio. She's your best friend's mother.*

"No. Seriously. Thanks, though."

She nodded. "I'd ask Hamilton, but . . ."

We stood for a moment like we both had something more to say. In case she didn't say her bit, I said mine.

"He's pretty torn up about everything," I told her. "Hamilton, I mean. About you and his uncle."

It was a gamble, but the worst I was going to get was a

polite good-bye and Land Rover exhaust in my face as she sped away. Instead I got a little more.

"I know this has been very difficult on him, and I'm glad you're here. Claude was just telling me—he was just saying how Hamilton needed friends around him right now. People he trusts. That he'll come around, in time."

I wasn't sure about that, but there was no harm in letting her think it.

"Claude really cares a great deal about him, Horatio. About this whole family. He's a dear, sweet man who saw me through a very difficult time. I know Hamilton disapproves, but Claude's made my life so much happier in these few months. I wish Hamilton could see that."

A blue jay landed on a stone vase overflowing with petunias and studied us. Mrs. Prince looked into my eyes, and I realized for the first time that I was actually taller than her now.

"I don't suppose he'd listen to you, would he?" she asked.

I scratched the back of my head, picturing Hamilton slumped over a chair in the entertainment room.

"I'm not sure how much he's really listening to anybody right now."

Mrs. Prince nodded. She put a hand on my arm and made me melt.

"It doesn't matter," she told me. "It's still good that you're here."

Down the driveway, an approaching car blared out the first few notes of "Dixie" and sent our blue jay flying. The very nice fantasy I was just starting to have again flew away with it. A Frankensteined Dodge Charger with more gray Bondo work than actual metal swerved up the gravel road, leaving a heavy cloud of dust and dirt in its wake. The car skidded to a stop behind Mrs. Prince's SUV, lurching as the driver let off the clutch without taking it out of gear.

Two good ole boys climbed out—through the doors, thankfully, not the windows—and made their way up to us on the steps. One of them was heavyset and wore a black Lynyrd Skynyrd tank top over his paunch. The other one was thin to the point of looking unhealthy, and sported a wispy goatee and a bowling shirt covered with images of a NASCAR driver. They were as colorful as Candy the Cowboy, but I was guessing this wasn't more of the help.

The thick one grinned through tobacco-stained teeth. "Howdy, Mizz Prince. Remember us?"

"Gilbert?" she asked. She turned to the other one. "Roscoe?"

The thin one gave the fat one a backhanded slap to the chest.

"Told you she'd remember us, huh?"

"Horatio, this is . . . Roscoe Grant and Gilbert Stern," she said. I noticed she was trying their names in reverse, which meant she didn't really remember them that well. "They're old friends of Hamilton's, from middle school. They live here in Denmark."

"No kidding," I said.

"Horatio? What's that? Some kind of French fairy name?" one of them asked.

"He was a Roman poet, actually."

"Same difference," the other one said with a grin.

"This is certainly a surprise," said Mrs. Prince.

"We came to see Hamilton."

"Cheer him up."

"You'll have to wake him up first," I told them. "He's asleep in the entertainment room."

"Entertainment room? Aw, sweet!"

The pair tapped their fists together in some kind of tepid high five and shuffled past us into the house. I blinked and waited for Mrs. Prince to close her mouth.

"Well," she said finally. "They've certainly changed since middle school."

"You never know," I told her. "They might still be *in* middle school."

I saw the flicker of a smile on Mrs. Prince's face, but it disappeared like dirty underwear when company comes.

"I'd better go or I'll be late. It was good to talk to you, Horatio."

"You too, Mrs. Prince."

The Land Rover drove off, and I stepped away from the house. The theater upstairs had probably already been taken over by Hamilton's surprise guests, and I had no desire to swap bass-fishing stories over a six-pack of Pabst Blue Ribbon. It was as good a time as any to check the messages on my cell, and I flipped it open as I walked down the drive.

No bars, no service. This wasn't roaming, it was disappearing.

An old yellow Jeep with the canvas top down came bobbing up the driveway, and I wondered if the Princes should start charging a toll. I spotted my red Cardinals hat through the windshield, and I waited as Olivia pulled to a stop next to me.

"Running away?" she asked. "Didn't you forget your teddy bear and your security blanket?"

"Just out catching a breath of fresh stink," I told her. "If you're looking to trade insults with your ex, he's passed out on a couch in the TV room. But you'll have to get through his two old NASCAR buddies Roscoe and Gilbert first."

"Dumb and Dumber? What are they doing here?"

"Watching pro wrestling on the big screen right about now, I'm guessing."

Olivia swung the Jeep off the road and turned it around so it was facing the other direction, toward town. She stopped beside me again and nodded to the empty seat beside her.

"My mother told me never to take rides from strangers," I told her.

She smirked. "Well. We'll just have to get to know each other a little better then, won't we?"

CHAPTER SEVEN

We cruised down winding East Tennessee back roads for fifteen, maybe twenty minutes, neither of us saying a word. The Jeep rattled a bit on the straightaways and the brakes squeaked in the turns, but it felt like we could climb one of the giant, sloping green mountains in the distance without losing so much as a lug nut. If there had ever been a stereo it was stripped out, but you wouldn't have wanted to listen to it anyway. There was plenty of music in the rush of air and the hint of running water in the near distance. The top was down, the doors were off, and there was nothing separating me from the swiftly passing landscape but a worn-out old seat belt. It was exhilarating.

The tires rat-tat-tatted across a modest wooden bridge with low railings, and Olivia pulled to a stop near the middle where the river passed underneath.

"You didn't have to stop," I told her. "We could just keep driving like this until it's time to go to college."

She knew I wasn't kidding and she smiled. She yanked on the emergency brake.

"Come on. I want to show you something."

I climbed out of the Jeep and came around to where she stood. Over the side, a gorgeous little river passed beneath us, one of those immaculate mountain streams where they film beer commercials.

"You said you'd like to see the Copenhagen River," she told me. "Here it is. This is what I'm fighting to save."

A fish swam by underneath—an actual honest-to-God fish the length of my entire arm.

"Ever been night fishing?" she asked me.

"I can probably count on one hand the number of times I've been *day* fishing. I didn't know there *was* another kind."

"Maybe you should join me up here one night."

"How can you see what you're doing?"

Olivia gave me a little smile. "Well, you have to use your hands a lot."

She worked one of those hands into the pocket of her tight jeans and pulled out a shiny new penny. She made sure I was watching, then dropped it into the water below. It flitted and twisted its way through the current, all the way to the round gray river rocks on the bottom.

"The river looks pretty clean to me," I told her. "Amazingly clean."

"That's because we're upstream of Elsinore."

Olivia climbed back in the Jeep, and I followed. We drove again, the river cutting in and out of the woods beside us like a happy dog. It was such a beautiful day you could almost ignore the terrible smell. Almost.

Then, if it was possible, the stench got worse. Olivia looked across the gear shift at me, making sure I noticed. The tears in my eyes were answer enough. She pulled off the main road and drove down an unmarked, overgrown dirt road that led to the river. A few yards away she cut the engine and nodded ahead. It reeked so bad, neither of us wanted to open our mouths to talk.

I poked my way through the bramble and the stunted trees until I caught sight of the water, or what passed for it. It looked like a river of Pepsi. A dark brown liquid churned up white froth as it broke against the rocks, and pallid clumps of foam roamed the surface like slugs. How anything could live in the murky depths below seemed impossible.

My eyes burned. "Ye gods and little fishes," I muttered.

Olivia was sensible enough to have brought a handkerchief to cover her mouth and her nose, but she was letting me experience the Copenhagen River full on. And why not? She had taken me to the river to be baptized into her religion, and now I was a total convert.

"Elsinore Paper is doing this?" I said, coughing.

She pointed to a roiling, bubbling part of the river, like a fountain of sewage erupting from the surface. From there, it was easy to trace the big industrial pipe that wound up into the woods toward the plant.

Olivia took my hand and led me back to the Jeep, where I slumped into my seat. All the thrill of driving down back roads with the top down was suddenly gone, replaced by an overpowering urge to spew chunks. She took it easy on the road as we left, and I avoided projectile vomiting as my nausea subsided.

"That was the most disgusting thing I've ever seen," I said when I could. "Or tasted." I smacked my lips and tongue, trying desperately to rid them of the aftertaste from the air. It was worse than when I was five and accidentally drank from a soda bottle filled with used motor oil.

"There's no way a company like Elsinore Paper would ever build on a river as small as the Copenhagen these days,"

Olivia told me. "A hundred years ago, it was a little paper plant on a little river. But Elsinore Paper grew, and the Copenhagen didn't. Today they'd build a plant this size on the Mississippi and dump the same crap they're dumping here, only the Mississippi is so big, it would blend in. Same crap, just harder to see. Here there's no way to hide it."

"How can they get away with it?"

"Who's going to stop them? Hamilton's dad said it would cost so much to run clean, he'd have to close down for good. That paper plant employs almost two thousand people, not to mention all the shops and restaurants that rely on those people having money to spend. There's only four thousand or so people in all of Denmark, Tennessee. How many of them do you think are gonna vote to make Elsinore clean up its act when that might mean losing their jobs?"

"You believe him? Mr. Prince? That he'd have to close the plant?"

"I think its BS. He could have cleaned up without closing. He just didn't want to spend the money when he didn't have to."

Olivia pulled into a combination gas station/convenience store/post office and angled the car so I could see where we were.

"What's this?" I asked.

"Its real name is Jackson Hollow, but everybody around here calls it Widowville."

Widowville was a tiny little row of broken-down houses and abandoned buildings. It dead-ended in an overgrown lot filled with rusted-out train cars. The four-way intersection at the heart of town didn't even warrant a stoplight, and the entire time we were there not one car came down the road.

"Somebody actually lives here?" I asked.

"About fifty people, maybe. A few more up in the hills. This town used to be where the woodcutters lived, back when the mill was small enough to still use wood from the surrounding area. Now they slice up parts of national parks out west and ship the lumber in by rail." Olivia leaned forward on the steering wheel. "There are families in this town that have worked for Elsinore Paper for three generations. Now they're paying for it. Almost all the men who worked for decades at Elsinore are dead."

"All of them? From what?"

"Cancer."

It was the second time that day someone had answered one of my questions with "cancer," and I was a bit spooked.

"There was a study done, a few years back," she told me. "Researchers came over from Duke, did a population study. They said the death rate from cancer was no different here than anywhere else in the country. But how many men got cancer after the doctors left? How many had already died not knowing what killed them? Seriously—where are all the men? There's just a handful left here. The new generations live over the mountain, away from the river. But these men worked their whole lives for that plant, spent their nights sleeping beside that river, and now they're gone. You can't tell me the river didn't make them sick."

"Surely they weren't drinking the water, though, were they?"

"God, no. That probably would have killed them right off. But where do you think these people get their water from? They pump it from the ground, from wells. Tell me that nasty river isn't feeding into the water table. Just ask the folks whose tap water comes out looking brown and smelling like rotten eggs. How long do you think they drank that stuff before it got discolored enough to see it?"

The door to the gas station/convenience store/post office jangled open behind us, and an old woman walked out with a loaf of bread and a plastic jug of water.

"Seen enough?" Olivia asked me, and I nodded.

Back in Denmark, Olivia swung into the parking lot of a greasy spoon. "Can you eat? It's my treat."

"I think I can keep it down," I told her.

The door squawked on the way inside, grinding against torn linoleum on the floor. The place had that dirty look old diners get from years of crumbs and grease, even though the tables looked clean enough to eat off of. The red vinyl seat cushions along the counter were dried out and cracked, and a few of the fluorescents on the ceiling flickered in prolonged death throes. A tired-looking old waitress—the same one who works in every diner in every town in every state across the country—was taking her smoke break underneath the No Smoking sign in the corner near the coffee machine. This hour of the afternoon, we were the only customers.

"Ya'll sit wherever you like," the ancient waitress croaked. "I'll be right there."

Olivia looked at me expectantly.

"What?" I said.

"Hamilton hates this place. He'd already be out the door, heading up to that chain restaurant on the interstate."

I shrugged. "You want the counter or a booth?"

Olivia slid into a booth, and for a moment I envied the taped-up seat cushion as she got comfortable. I crawled into my side and leaned back against the grimy window. The E in the word "EATS" cast a slanting backward shadow across our table.

The waitress appeared next to us, depositing glasses of

water like they do now only in dives and five-star restaurants. "Hey honey," she said, looking right at me but clearly addressing Olivia. "What'll ya have?"

"Hamburger, onion rings, and a Diet Coke," Olivia said without looking at a menu.

"Same here, only make mine fries and a root beer instead, if you've got it."

"Cheese or curly?"

"Curly."

That seemed to be all the information the waitress required, and she slid away from the table with a lingering look at Olivia.

"You a regular?" I asked.

"Regular enough," she said. "Pie's good."

Drinks appeared in front of us, and the waitress gave us our space as she smoked another cigarette and waited on our order to come up.

"So everybody lets Elsinore poison that river because they need the money?"

"Basically," Olivia said. She sipped her water. "I tried for two years to get Hamilton's father to do something about it. He said there were fish still living in that water, that he fished it all the time. He was as full of crap as that river."

"What about the government? The Environmental Protection Agency? Wouldn't they be all over this?"

"Are you kidding? The EPA is in the state's pocket. Tennessee doesn't want to see that plant shut down any more than the people of Denmark. They need the tax revenue. Besides, Elsinore has passed every one of its water quality tests."

"You're kidding."

Our elderly attendant slid our plates in front of us. My hamburger was huge, piled high with lettuce and tomato, and surrounded by a mountain of curly fries. The taste of the river was quickly replaced by a gloriously greasy aroma.

Olivia shook her head, taking a huge bite of hamburger and chasing it with Diet Coke. "Uh-uh. But I know how they did it. They just took samples from the river where unpolluted streams fed in from the mountains. That way there's still pollution, so the EPA knows it's from the river, but the fresh water dilutes the junk and makes it look better than it really is."

"They can't tell it's polluted by just looking at it?"

"They're never gonna come all the way out here," Olivia said through a mouthful. "Would you?"

"You must have been pretty pissed. At Hamilton's father, I mean."

Olivia shrugged. "Well, yeah. He was poisoning Denmark. He knew it, and he didn't care. And you can bet the only water he ever drank came from a bottle. He should have had to drink poison like the rest of us. Then he'd have changed his tune."

I chewed in silence. By his own account, Rex Prince *had* been poisoned. The question was, did a devastatingly attractive teenaged Denmark girl with access to his house see that poetic justice was served with his dinner?

"You know, I heard it was cancer that killed him after all," Olivia confided.

"No kidding."

"Yeah. I'd think it really *was* the water if he ever drank it. Water, I mean. The only thing I ever saw him drink was whisky, and lots of it."

"Are you saying he was an alcoholic?"

"Calling Mr. Prince an alcoholic would be like saying the Copenhagen is dirty. It doesn't begin to cover it." She raised her glass. "Like father, like son."

It was nice to know I wasn't the only person who had apparently given Hamilton a hard time about his drinking problem. I wondered if that was part of what had come between them, and why I didn't ride him harder about it. Maybe that was the difference between like and love.

As she drove me home, I remembered Olivia standing there in the rain protesting Elsinore Paper where no one but Hamilton could see her. At first I had thought that Elsinore's pollution was just a convenient knife to stick in her ex-boyfriend for spite, but it was clear her passion for the cause went well beyond the fury of a woman scorned. But just how far did it go?

We pulled up in front of the Prince estate just before dusk. I climbed out of the Jeep and Olivia kept the motor running.

"Was there some message you want me to take to Hamilton?" I asked her.

"Yeah," she said. "Tell him I hope a tree falls on him."

"You really came all this way out here just to rag on him?"

"Who says I came all this way to talk to Hamilton?"

Olivia threw the Jeep into gear and sped off, and I prayed to the Norse gods of Denmark I wasn't falling in love with a murderer.

CHAPTER EIGHT

—💀—

I half hoped Olivia Mendelsohn would drive up the next morning and whisk me away to someplace exotic like Mexico or Canada or Albuquerque. Instead the only invitation I got was to play a racing game with Roscoe and Gilbert, who had apparently been given guest rooms. I took a pass. In the shower, I wondered just who exactly had invited Bo and Luke Duke to the house, and why. Mrs. Prince had seemed just as surprised to see them drive up as I was, and Hamilton had been giving them a wide berth. That left Claude as the cruise director, but I didn't see the angle yet. After a quick powder at the boudoir in my room I felt like a new man and went looking for Hamilton.

I knocked softly on his door expecting him to still be asleep, and I was right. Hamilton was crashed out on his bed wearing the clothes he had on last night. An empty glass sat overturned on his bedside table. I didn't need him right now anyway; it was his computer I was after.

Ford Branff was due to visit today, and I wanted to know more about him. Money is always a good motive in murder mysteries, and if Branff was proposing a takeover of Elsinore

Paper, we were talking a lot of money indeed. It seemed like a long shot that he could have orchestrated the death of Hamilton's father from wherever it was he lived, but I didn't want to count anyone out just yet.

Ford N. Branff, I learned, was the nation's most eligible media mogul. While the business pages were busy speculating on which companies he might acquire, the society pages were guessing which woman he might acquire. So far there were no women on the radar, but plenty of businesses. From his humble beginnings owning a lonely little community television station and a daily paper in Charlotte, North Carolina, he now owned seven papers, twelve television channels, and eight radio station groups throughout the southeast. And he wasn't done. There were reports of pending acquisitions in Virginia and Georgia too. Branff was branffing out.

There was no connection between Branff and Elsinore—at least none that I could find. After that I checked in on my dad's fantasy baseball team and skimmed boingboing.net. Fifteen minutes later I was lost in a gallery of Japanese robot pictures and had to close the browser before I spent all day surfing.

My stomach told me it was time for a little something and I set out on an expedition to discover the stairs. I heard the doorbell ring and I homed in on it like sonar. As I came down the stairs, one of the hired help was opening the door for the very man I had just Googled. Branff was a sharp-looking fellow, but his photo on the "Fifty Young Lions of Business 2006" list didn't do him justice. He swooped into the Prince castle modeling the latest in business-casual perfect. His fitted dress shirt was the color a tag would have called "espresso" instead of brown, and had a satiny smooth sheen. The pants looked easy to travel in, and sported a chalk-stripe design that gave them a sophisticated flair and an element of whimsy. Or at least that's what I imagined the Banana Republic catalog said. If we hadn't been a hundred million miles from the nearest city, he could have passed for metrosexual.

Mrs. Prince was just coming to the door, but I beat her there. Branff spied me coming down the stairs.

"Is that Hamilton?" He pulled off his burnished-gold sunglasses and stepped inside. "You don't look a thing like your mother!"

"I'm the black sheep of the family," I told him.

Mrs. Prince walked into Branff's open arms and kissed him on the cheek as they embraced. "It's so good to see you again, Ford." They held the pose just long enough for me to feel the weirdness, and then separated. Mrs. Prince smiled at me.

"Ford, this is Horatio Wilkes, a friend of Hamilton's from school. He's staying with us for part of the summer."

Branff laughed. It was much more subtle and practiced than Claude's, but still fake. He held out his hand.

"No wonder you don't look like Trudy. Horatio, huh? That's a funny name."

I shook his hand. "Don't worry. It's not giving yours any competition."

He held my hand a second longer than he should have, trying to figure out how I thought we were such good buds I could say mean things about him already. When he couldn't figure it out, he smiled awkwardly and let go.

"I hope I'll get to meet the real Hamilton Prince Jr.," he joked with Mrs. Prince. "I like to think he could have been my son instead."

"You should say that to Hamilton," I told him. Then the Branff would really hit the fan.

Mrs. Prince put a delicate finger to a button on an intercom and said, "Hamilton?" into it.

There was a brief pause, then a crackle, a hum, and a "What."

"We have a visitor. Ford Branff. I'd like you to meet him."

Mrs. Prince released the button with a click, and waited. When there was no response, she turned to her old college flame. "Come on in, Ford. We have a lot of catching up to do."

She led Branff in the general direction of the kitchen, and I followed. Mrs. Prince showed him into one of the hundred or so sitting rooms in the place, and Candy the Cowboy appeared in the doorway wearing a cow-print shirt with tassels and tight blue jeans. He waited for Mrs. Prince's orders with an impossible smile.

"Candy, could you bring us some refreshments, please? Claude and Hamilton will be joining us as well."

"Of course, *señora*."

Mrs. Prince went into the parlor with Branff, and Candy and I met each other's eyes at five paces. I usually go out of my way to be nice to anybody paid to wait on me, but Candy was different. For one thing, he didn't act like any servant I had ever met. For another, he had pushed my buttons without provocation yesterday, and I couldn't let that go.

"No bandana today?" I asked. "I'm disappointed. Did they go out of fashion so quickly?"

He kept the cow-patty-eating smile, but his eyes narrowed. Today he decided he'd win by not rising to my bait, and he turned on his heel and strutted away toward the kitchen. I tagged along.

"You know what would really make that ensemble sing?" I said. "Chaps."

Still nothing. But I thought he was maybe working the strut a little more for my benefit. As we entered the kitchen he put a hand to his behind, silently telling me I could kiss it. I laughed and went to the refrigerator, waving off multiple offers of assistance from the other servants working in the kitchen. I found a bag of fresh bagels and was just trying to sneak one into a toaster before someone could offer to butter it for me when Hamilton walked in. He'd made a remarkable recovery from the corpse I'd seen in the bed earlier, and he'd even deigned to put on a new shirt.

"He's here?" Hamilton asked. "Banff?"

"Branff," I corrected him.

Hamilton grabbed a donut from the ever-present tray of sweets.

"What's he doing here? Or doesn't he care she's already married again?"

"I suspect he's here about the takeover."

"Good. Let's get it over with," Hamilton said. He left for the parlor while I waited for my bagel to get crispy. Candy was hard at work making some kind of cocktail out of gin and Rose's lime juice. I guess it was happy hour twenty-four/ seven here at the Dew Drop Inn. A servant put a plate in front of me before I could find one for myself, and I ended up walking back down the hall at the same time as Candy. I thought about riding him, but I ate my bagel instead.

I skulked into the smallish sitting room while Candy made a grand entrance, offering Branff a drink from his tray with a flourish. Branff took the one with the lime sticking out of it. Hamilton and Claude had joined Mrs. Prince to welcome their guest, and the two adults took martinis. Hamilton had to settle for a soda. I settled into an out-of-the-way chair in the corner and noshed my bagel while I watched the show.

"Candy makes the best martinis. I see you still drink gimlets, Ford," Mrs. Prince said with a laugh. "How you can drink those things?"

"Old habits die hard," Branff said. I guessed there was supposed to be something more to that, something only Mrs. Prince understood.

Claude was unamused. "So you're here about the hostile takeover, then?"

Branff grimaced. "Oh, I dislike the term 'hostile takeover.' It's so . . . bellicose."

Claude frowned.

"Belligerent," Hamilton said. "Aggressive. Warlike. Buy a dictionary."

Claude scowled at Hamilton, but he had bigger fish to poison.

"Trudy and I have discussed this. We're not interested in selling."

"But you haven't even heard my terms," Branff said.

"We don't have to hear them," Claude said.

"Don't you? Wouldn't your board of trustees be interested to learn, for example, that you're losing market share? You spent a lot of money to court Guerrero Greeting Cards, and they ended up going to Black Forest Paper instead. Not only that, I understand you're about to lose Doodle Stationery as well."

Claude turned red. "How can you— That's confidential! Where are you getting your information?"

Branff settled back into his chair and sipped his gimlet. "There's also the small matter of Elsinore's impact on the environment, which, it appears, is not so secret." Branff withdrew a neatly folded orange flyer from his back pocket and handed it to Claude. "I found this in the window of a business downtown."

From across the room, the only words I could make out on the paper were: "Brown-Water Rafting Race."

"Olivia Mendelsohn," Claude muttered.

"It's quite clever really," Branff said. "A play on white-water rafting, I suppose. But since the Copenhagen is brown now—"

Claude wadded the flyer up and threw it into the unlit fireplace. "That girl's been nagging us for a long time, but she's the only really vocal one. It's nothing to worry about."

"Not yet, maybe," said Branff. "But I'm in the communications business, Mr. Prince. I know the power of bad publicity. One good stunt, one good human-interest story that gets picked up by a local news crew and then syndicated to the national media, and you're ruined."

"Is that some kind of a threat?" Claude asked.

Branff shrugged it off, but it was a threat, pure and simple. And a good one too.

"Think of it as professional advice," Branff said. "From one businessman to another."

Claude chewed on this new development. Branff drank his gimlet. Mrs. Prince looked uncomfortable.

"I'm willing to offer you a fair price," Branff told them. He looked at Mrs. Prince. "*More* than a fair price, considering the money I'd have to invest to clean up the river and the public relations nightmare you're cultivating."

"You mean it *can* be cleaned up?" I asked.

Suddenly everyone turned and noticed I was in the room with them.

"You can clean up the plant and still afford to run it?"

"My engineers tell me we could do it," Branff said. He redirected the sales pitch to the people who mattered. "If we use a non-chlorine-based bleaching process instead, the plant can run clean. And cheaper, in the long run, after the initial costs of replacing the equipment, of course."

I nearly choked on my poppy seed bagel. So Hamilton's father *had* been feeding the town a line about having to pollute or shut down. The poisoned look I was giving the collective Prince family went completely unnoticed.

"This isn't about cleaning up the plant, and it isn't about doing us any favors," said Claude. "What I can't figure is why you—"

"How much?" Hamilton asked. It was the first time he'd said anything at all.

"What?" asked Branff.

"How much. Money. How much to buy Elsinore."

Branff blinked, then recovered nicely.

"Six and a half billion dollars."

That number danced a little jig before everyone's eyes, including my own. Claude sat back in his chair, thinking about what he could buy with his share of the cash. Like maybe a Major League Baseball team or three.

"I have seven newspapers," Branff said, "soon to be nine. They cost me a fortune in paper every day. I acquire Elsinore, we switch over to all newsprint, and Branff Communications cuts out the middle man. It's called vertical acquisition. And you, Prince family, you get the proverbial 'golden handshake.'"

"Sell it," Hamilton said. He stood to leave. "Sell it all."

"No," said Claude. "Your father wouldn't have sold the plant, and neither will I. I've done too much, come too far to just hand everything away now—"

"*You've* done too much?" said Hamilton. "You!? What did you ever do but mooch off my dad and wait around for him to die so you could hop into his chair?" He shot a look at his mother. "And his *bed*."

Mrs. Prince stood and reached for her son's arm. "Hamilton, we're not—"

Hamilton pulled away, knocking over what was undoubtedly a priceless Ming dynasty vase with a lampshade on top. It shattered into a dozen pieces against the hearth, and Hamilton kicked the little end table for good measure.

"Hamilton!" Mrs. Prince cried.

Hamilton turned on his uncle. "My dad didn't slave his whole life away on this effing place so you could just take right over when he was gone."

"Elsinore isn't his. It belongs to this family. Your great-great-great-grandfather built a paper mill here a hundred—"

"My father *made* Elsinore what it is today. He took a pissant little paper company and made it into a multinational corporation while you did two things: jack and squat." Hamilton calmed down suddenly. "Unless you did something else to get where you are today."

Claude stood, dwarfing Hamilton with his bulk. His voice got as icy as Antarctica.

"You know, I used to get the same lecture from your father. 'I worked hard to get where I am today, Claude. Nobody gets rich overnight, Claude. You've got to finish what you start, Claude.' Well, maybe I finally listened. I put in the time and effort, and now I'm here and your father's not, and I'm not going to let *anybody* take away what I've earned."

Claude's outburst settled on the room like snow, and I shivered. What was Claude saying? Did he envy and resent his brother enough to turn his advice against him and slowly poison him, for once in his life seeing something through to its end?

Hamilton must have had a similar thought, because he stepped backward, clearly frightened by his uncle. He bumped into the lamp and end table that matched the one he'd already destroyed, and his fear quickly turned to anger. He turned and did to the table what he must have wanted to do to Claude right then, reducing it to a pile of splinters.

"Stop!" said Mrs. Prince. "Hamilton!"

"Hamilton, have you been drinking again?" Claude asked.

Hamilton spun on his stepfather. "What if I have?" he demanded. I knew Hamilton had had too much to drink last night, but the only thing he'd had for breakfast was a donut and a hangover. He pretended he was drunk anyway, going Bruce Lee on what was left of the lamp.

Ford N. Branff swirled his gimlet, looking not the least bit surprised at the family meltdown he was witnessing. "Perhaps I've come at a bad time," he said. He was a little too amused for my tastes. Hamilton's too, apparently.

"Yeah," he told Branff. "A little sooner and you could have gotten my mom in the bargain."

Claude told Hamilton to go to his room and Hamilton told Claude to go to hell. Neither of them obliged. Hamilton stalked out to simmer someplace else and Mrs. Prince left in tears. Again. This time Claude followed his wife, his "needy woman" antennae twitching.

That left me and the Banana Republic model.

"Still like to think Hamilton could be your son?" I asked Branff.

A team of servants—including Candy the Cowboy—appeared out of nowhere and immediately began cleaning up the debris from Hamilton's rampage. I crossed to the fireplace to retrieve the crumpled brown-water rafting flyer before they could whisk it away. In fifteen minutes the room would be wiped clean, and this little episode would only be a legend, whispered about quietly over bowls of gruel in the staff dungeon.

Ford Branff stood and handed his empty glass to Candy.

"Please let Mrs. Prince know that I'm staying at the motel by the interstate," Branff said. "You know the one?"

"*Sí,*" said Candy. I noticed he didn't waste one of his plastic smiles on Branff.

"Room 112," Branff added.

"*Sí, señor. Muchas gracias.*"

Branff frowned at Candy and walked out of the room without telling me good-bye. And here I thought we were bonding.

"You want me to take that back to the kitchen?" a young female servant asked. She nodded at my empty breakfast plate.

"No thanks. I got it."

She smiled and I smiled and left her to her dirty work, wondering again about what it took to keep picking up after children and not be their mother.

I also wondered how Candy knew Branff drank gimlets without ever asking.

CHAPTER NINE

Hamilton disappeared after playing Godzilla in the parlor, and I didn't want to spend all day searching the house for him. I was more interested in Olivia's brownwater rafting race. I knew now, from what Branff had said, that she was right about the Princes jerking Denmark around on the pollution thing. I had no intention of riding a raft down that skanky river, but I figured I'd put in an appearance for moral support. I also knew it would get me points with Olivia. I hated myself for being so sycophantic, but she was the kind of girl you liked to have points with on account, just in case.

I didn't know what to make of Claude's revelation. I could see now that Hamilton was right; Claude resented his brother and coveted his success. But that resentment didn't mean he had murdered him—it just meant he wasn't sad his brother was dead.

I smoothed Olivia's crinkled flyer again on the car seat beside me and took a left, heading down to the river. It was already eighty-five degrees outside by eleven thirty that morning, and the air was so heavy with humidity I debated turning on my windshield wipers. I threw the air conditioner on full-blast and felt my 1986 Volvo 240 gasp under the strain. My car was big and boxy and white. It was older than I was, and had been handed down to me through no less than three sisters. I loved it like it was one.

I thought I'd followed the directions wrong when I got to the raft race site. There were only a couple of cars parked along the road above the river, but I saw Olivia's Jeep hiding among the underbrush and found a safe place to tether the Volvo. I started to sweat the minute I stepped out of the car, and the steep descent to the riverbank was work and made it worse. The smell from the pollution was overpowering too, and the air was so thick it felt like I was drinking the river. The only place I had been with humidity this bad was St. Louis last summer, visiting my dad. At least there the air soup only tasted like asphalt and motor oil.

Olivia stood talking with a man and a woman on a small, flat bank beside the Willy Wonka–like river. A couple of big yellow inflatable rafts, the kind tourists go flopping down rivers in, sat in the grass beneath a string of little colored pennants and a sign that said: "First Annual Brown-Water Rafting Race." Olivia caught sight of me coming and wrapped up her conversation with the other two. They shook hands with her and nodded hello to me as they left.

"Brown-water racers?" I asked Olivia.

"Friends from town. The few who actually support cleaning up the river."

From her clinging shirt and the way her hair was plastered to the back of her neck, it looked like Olivia had already been out there awhile. At least my Cardinals hat was helping keep things under control.

I nodded at her brown-water rafting sign. "You know, you're really not supposed to say 'first annual.' Nothing's annual until you've done it a couple of years in a row."

"Thanks," said Olivia. She put a hand in her back pocket like she was going for a wallet. "Do you charge for editorial services, or is this one gratis?"

I smiled. "Call it a donation. So, am I early or late?"

"You're right on time. Start letting the air out of that raft over there."

"No takers, then?"

Olivia released the stopper from one of the rafts and started to roll the air out. "Nobody was going to come down here and raft on the Copenhagen," she told me. "They'd be crazy to. Hell, the water would probably eat the bottom of these rafts up like acid anyway. I just did it for the publicity."

I looked around for the publicity, but I didn't see any.

"All right, all right," she said. "I was hoping someone from the *Daily Dane* would come out and cover it, but they ignored me like always. It got mentioned in the calendar, though, and I had flyers up around town. I figure it's something if I can just keep reminding them the river's here."

"The *Daily Dane*?" I asked.

"Denmark's little newspaper."

I had my raft half-empty now, and I hefted the rolled-up part up under my arms and squeezed. Sweat poured down to the small of my back.

"You'd think the smell would be enough to remind them."

Olivia sat on what was left of her inflated raft. "It's not. But it looks like I got through to at least one person."

At first I thought she meant me, but then I saw where she was looking. On the road above us, Hamilton was watching from behind the window of his SUV. When he saw we'd spotted him he punched it, screeching away in a cloud of rock and dust.

"You seem to be doing an awful lot of work just to reach one person over and over again," I told her.

She picked up an armload of paddles. "Come on. Help me take this stuff to my Jeep."

We stowed everything in the back of Olivia's Jeep and she nodded for me to join her. I didn't much care where we were headed, but Olivia had someplace in mind. We climbed up and up, into the hills and mountains above Denmark, without either of us saying a word. The asphalt led to a gravel road that eventually became two dirt tracks, and then no kind of road at all. The Jeep bumped and bounced and came to a stop. Olivia hopped out and I followed. I hadn't noticed it when the Jeep was moving, but the air was cooler here and not as muggy. There was actually a breeze, and as I smelled the scents of pine and hydrangea I realized we had risen above something else up here: the stink from the Elsinore Paper Plant.

Olivia pushed through some brush and we emerged onto a rock bluff about the size of one of those big yellow rafts. It was mostly flat, with a bit of a slope out toward the edge where it plunged into an amazing view of Denmark, the mountains, and, in the distance, the belching smokestacks of Elsinore. Olivia sat on the rock, and I found a place next to her. She took in a deep breath, and I let her have her moment of Zen.

"You were right, you know," I said finally. "About the paper plant being able to clean up their act. The bastards just don't want to spend the money."

Olivia nodded like she'd always known. She hugged her knees to her chest and kept looking at that view.

"Nice spot," I said. "I think I can see my house from here."

"Hamilton brought me up here. On our first date." She laid her head on her knees, facing me but not looking at me. "And lots of times after that," she said.

I tossed a decaying pine cone over the edge.

"You know how you saw him write a poem to me once?" Olivia asked. "It wasn't the only one. After he went away to school, he wrote me a new poem every day. In actual letters, not in e-mails or anything. That's not the kind of thing you do for a summer fling, is it?"

"Doesn't seem like it, no."

"He could be really sweet like that, you know? I'd go to the mailbox and there'd be one almost every day. On really beautiful paper."

"Probably Elsinore paper," I told her.

She laughed, but I could hear tears in it. "Yeah. It probably was," she said. "The bastard."

It was her time, her place, and I let her go where she wanted.

"I really thought he loved me. And I loved him too."

I didn't question her use of past tense. I'd already edited her once today. Olivia sniffed and tried to dry an eye on her shoulder so I couldn't tell she was crying, and I pretended not to see her.

"So I don't know if you know this," I told her, "but Hamilton's a good pitcher. Really good. He could probably get a scholarship somewhere, even though he doesn't need it."

Olivia didn't say she was interested, but she didn't say she wasn't, so I kept talking.

"So one time our sophomore year, Hamilton's pitching this

amazing game—a perfect game through seven innings. You know what a perfect game is? No batter from the other team ever gets to first base. No walks, no hits, no errors. It's practically impossible. There have only been like seventeen perfect games in the *history* of Major League Baseball."

"I get it," she said.

"Okay, so I come up to hit in our half of the inning, and the catcher says something about Hamilton that I don't like, and I say something about the catcher's mother that he doesn't like."

"Not *you*," she joked.

"The next thing I know, the ball's coming in high and tight. I try to duck, but the ball catches my helmet and knocks me to the ground. The benches cleared, but nobody did anything stupid. I know how to take a free base in a tight game, so I got myself up without dusting myself off and headed down to first without a fight."

"Of course you did," said Olivia.

"The other team wasn't after me, anyway. They were trying to rattle Hamilton, get him thinking about plunking somebody in retaliation and break up the perfect game. The umpire gave both teams a warning too: The next pitcher who hit a batter was going to get thrown out. In between innings, Coach Wormsley pulled Hamilton aside and reminded him we only had a one-run lead and couldn't afford to put any base runners on. As his best friend and his catcher, I told him only an idiot would give up a chance at history.

"Hamilton said he agreed with both of us. I thought he still might throw at somebody, but he didn't. Instead he goes out that next inning and absolutely blows them away. We didn't score in our half of the inning, and Hamilton ran to the mound with only three outs to go in the ninth inning and a chan[ce to] make the nightly news—maybe even SportsCenter. He ta[kes] the perfect game through nine and two-thirds innings— twenty-six men up, twenty-six men down—and number twenty-seven steps to the plate: the pitcher who plunked me. The easiest out on the team. I put down the sign for a fastball away, and what does Hamilton do?"

Olivia smiled. "He hits him."

"Eighty-mile-an-hour fastball right in the middle of his back. Sounded like somebody hitting a melon with a sledge-hammer. The guy's legs went out from under him and he didn't get up for five minutes. Hamilton lost his perfect game and got tossed to boot. The coach was furious. Me, I never laughed so hard in all my life. I wanted to be mad at him too, but I couldn't be. He wouldn't have nailed that guy if he had hit anybody but me. I know it." I smiled. "He could be sweet like that, you know?"

Olivia laughed. "Is that why you can still stand to be around him?"

"That's part of it. There's other stuff too. Besides, you don't walk away from your best friend just because he's going through a tough time."

Olivia looked at the ground.

"Hey, I didn't mean—he's been a real dillweed to you," I told her. "You've got every right to hate him."

"He walked away from me first."

"I know. And if you ask me, he was the world's biggest fool to—"

Olivia leaned in and tried to steal first base. I pulled away before she could kiss me, and she sat up and looked at me like I was crazy. Maybe I was.

e can't," I told her. "As much as I want to."

"You think I'm doing this just to hurt Hamilton?"

"No. But it *would* hurt him, and I can't do that to him."

Olivia spat out an unhappy laugh and shook her head.

"You ever let yourself do anything wrong, Horatio Wilkes?"

"What's that supposed to mean?"

"You don't drink, you don't smoke, you won't kiss your best friend's ex-girlfriend. I'll bet you wait for the light at crosswalks and always drive the speed limit."

"I break the rules plenty," I told her.

"Sure you do. So let me guess. Big family, right?"

I didn't know where she was going, and I frowned.

"Youngest child, Mom and Dad are already over it from bringing up all your brothers and sisters, so they give you a pass. How am I doing?"

She seemed to like the sound of her own voice, so I let her talk.

"But instead of having fun, you make your own rules—tougher even than they would have made for you if they cared. You become your own parent."

"I get along great with my parents."

"Of course you do. They've treated you like an adult since the day you were born. That's part of the problem."

"You've been reading too many self-help books," I told her.

"Yeah, well, maybe you haven't been reading enough."

Where the hell did she get off psychoanalyzing me? I wanted to get up and walk away, but I liked this girl. But if I liked her so much, why had I stopped her from kissing me? *Damn it.* How had I messed this up so badly?

"I think you better take me back to my car," I said, and I got no argument from Olivia.

We didn't talk again on the ride down the mountain, but this time it was for a different reason. She let me out and I stood by my car and she sat in hers and we both could have said something right then to fix things, but we didn't. Finally she looked away and eased out onto the road, still wearing my cap and still looking pretty. I got in my steaming hot car and banged my fist against the steering wheel while the air conditioner blasted me in the face.

CHAPTER TEN

—☠—

I drove five miles an hour above the posted speed limit through town and took a rolling stop at a stop sign, even if Olivia wasn't there to appreciate the effort. She had said some things that rang pretty true when I thought about them, so I chose not to think about them. It was her pain talking anyway. I was the second guy in as many months to make it clear he wouldn't have her as a girlfriend. I tried to tell myself that she was still in love with Hamilton and that she would have just hated herself more in the long run for making out with me, but somehow that was little consolation.

Up ahead I saw a large potted plant staggering away from a familiar SUV. I pulled off into the small parking lot of what looked like an old mechanic's shop. The SUV and the legs belonged to Hamilton's mom; I didn't know who owned the plant.

I got out of my car. "Can I give you a hand with that, Mrs. Prince?"

"Horatio?" she asked, trying to place me from the sound of my voice.

"Here," I said. I reached my arms around the big vase and

brushed something soft and supple as I wrestled control of the plant. *Best friend's mom. Best friend's mom.*

Either the pot was made of lead or the Audrey II inside it had recently devoured a small cow. "Whoa," I said, shifting its weight until I could handle it. "Okay, where to?"

"You're such a dear. Just inside, in the lobby."

I couldn't see anything in front of me, so I had to take Mrs. Prince's word that the hot little room she led me to was any kind of lobby. After a bit of negotiation I put the plant where she wanted it and was able to stand up and see the place. It *was* an old mechanic's shop, but it had been converted into a small playhouse. The waiting area had a neat homemade concession stand/ticket table on one side and a small unisex bathroom on the other. Through the door into what was once the garage I could see rows of wooden theater seats bolted to risers.

"The community theater?" I asked between breaths.

"The Denmark Players," Mrs. Prince said.

One of the actors said hello to her in passing as he made his way inside. A sign on the wall advertised their upcoming performance. *"Rosencrantz and Guildenstern Are Dead,"* I read aloud.

"Do you know it?"

"I've seen the movie, but I've never seen it onstage."

"Oh, then you must come!" Mrs. Prince said, putting her hands on my shoulders. She liked to touch people, I noticed. "We'll make it a night at the theater, all of us."

I guessed that meant she'd bring Claude and I'd bring Hamilton. I didn't much like that combination, but Mrs. Prince was hard to say no to.

"Did you have anything else you needed help with?" I asked her.

Turns out the frodis had brothers, and I spent the better part of the next half hour playing pony to Mrs. Prince's plants. The whole time I was working, I wondered again if she had anything at all to do with her husband's death. She seemed so nice and considerate and harmless. But I also couldn't help picturing Hamilton's father from the videotape. That drained, white face, his horrible pockmarked skin. What was it he had said? That he had tried to keep his illness from his wife? But there was no way to hide that face. She *had* to know something was wrong. So why let him think she didn't notice? Or did Mrs. Prince let him pretend there was nothing wrong because she was the one poisoning him?

I put the last plant where she wanted it and Mrs. Prince put a hand on my arm.

"I can't tell you what a help you've been. Here. Sit. I'll get you something to drink and we can watch some of the rehearsal. Unless you have somewhere you need to be."

I told her I didn't and sat down a few rows up from the floor, which doubled as the theater stage. A handful of actors were stretching their legs, mouthing silent dialogue, cleansing their auras, or whatever it is actors do to get ready to perform. They didn't seem to care that I was watching them, which was, I guess, what made them actors. Mrs. Prince came back with a pair of water bottles and sat down beside me.

It was a golden opportunity to get answers to some of my questions about the death of Rex Prince, but that wasn't an easy conversation to start. "Gee Mrs. Prince, I was just wondering, did you help Claude kill your husband so the two of you could take over the paper plant?" While I was debating a witty entrée, she started the conversation for me.

"Horatio, do you have any idea what's wrong with Hamilton?"

I leaned back and put my feet up on the chair in front of me.

"I know he's unhappy about my marriage to Claude," she told me. "But it seems like there's something else. I've never seen him act this way before. So . . ."

"Out of control?"

"Yes." She stared at her water bottle and I took a deep breath.

"I think he still has a lot of questions about his father's death."

"Really? But we told him everything we knew. We didn't keep anything from him—"

"What about the way Hamilton's dad looked at the end? His face and his skin?"

Mrs. Prince put a trembling hand to her mouth and gasped. "But how did he—oh, no wonder he hates me." She started to cry, and I started to think I ought to carry a handkerchief. I certainly had a way of getting women to turn on the water-works lately.

"It was all Claude's idea," she said through her tears, and for a minute I thought she was confessing. "Rex didn't want me to know he was sick, but how could I not see it every time I looked at him? We both knew he was very sick. His skin turned gray, his hair turned white. It was like he aged forty years in four months. By the end he looked like a ghost."

She was right about that.

"But Claude said that if Rex wanted to pretend he wasn't sick, why shouldn't I play along? Rex was going to doctors, doing everything he could to get better, so what was the point of bringing it up? He didn't want to talk about it and I didn't want to talk about it. I'm ashamed to say it, but—but I just wanted to pretend it wasn't happening too. Claude told me that I should just enjoy whatever time I had left with him instead, and that's what I did."

If I had watched someone I loved slowly die—like one of my parents or my sisters—I would have cursed the doctors and howled at the moon. I couldn't imagine saying nothing, *doing* nothing, and I knew Hamilton would have been the same way.

"Is that why you didn't tell him? Hamilton?"

Mrs. Prince wiped the tears from her eyes before they could ruin her mascara. "He just would have come home from school, made a big deal over it. And the last thing his father needed was a reminder that he was ill. And I thought it would save Hamilton some of the pain. I guess I was wrong."

It was a little hard to believe she and Hamilton's father had never talked about it, but at least I had her answer.

"Claude was a real help to you then, wasn't he?"

"He was everything to me. When Rex would go to work, Claude would come over and let me cry on his shoulder. He was a rock, and I clung to him. He helped get me through everything with the illness." Mrs. Prince tightened her already tight bottle cap. "Then, after Rex died, Claude confessed how he'd always loved me, ever since Rex brought me home from college. He took me to a bluff high above town, the same place Rex took me the first time I came to Denmark, and he asked me to be his wife."

"Yeah, I understand that's a popular spot," I told her.

Mrs. Prince turned to me. "It made a kind of sense, him taking me up there to that place I had always associated with Rex. Rex had been such a great part of my life, and now he was gone, and I felt like if I didn't have something to fill that hole I couldn't go on living. And here was dear, sweet Claude. Claude, who had helped me so much. Claude, who already knew me and loved me. The only other person who might have helped was Hamilton, and he was away at school."

"You can't blame him for that," I told her.

"I don't, Horatio. I don't blame him for anything." She looked away. "I don't know. I don't even know why I'm telling you any of this. Am I making any sense?"

I got what she was saying, even if I couldn't see myself doing it.

"I really thought I might kill myself," Mrs. Prince told me. "Claude saved me from that. I mean, he didn't rush in and knock a bottle of pills out of my hand or anything. But having someone like him in my life let me keep going."

I nodded, and Mrs. Prince leaned over and hugged me. It was a strange kind of luck I had when beautiful women I couldn't touch kept throwing themselves at me with such abandon.

Mrs. Prince gave me a separation squeeze and pulled away. "You're a good listener, Horatio."

"Thanks. I'm on the Wittenberg Listening Team, so I get a lot of practice," I said.

She laughed and I smiled and we both relaxed. So, where were all the nice, beautiful women who *weren't* murder suspects? Because as much as I wanted to dismiss Trudy Prince from any complicity in her husband's death, nothing she told me had necessarily exonerated her. It could all be a sob story, meant to make people think she was nothing more than an innocent, grieving widow. And covering up the way Hamilton's dad looked those last few months still didn't sit right with me.

Down below us, the Denmark Players had dispensed with some rescheduling and announcements, and they were setting up for one of the later parts of the play. There was some tricky technical business to the scene, and the lights kept going off and on. Suddenly, in the corner, what had once appeared to be a solid wall became transparent, and in the darkness the spotlight caught the silhouettes of two dummies, swinging from ropes like they'd been hanged.

"There, what do you think of that?" a tech guy asked from the darkness.

I thought it was creepy, and if I believed in that kind of stuff I might have thought it was a bad omen. How had I let myself get dragged into all this? There must have been a moment, at the beginning, when I could have said no. But somehow I missed it.

CHAPTER ELEVEN

— 💀 —

Roscoe and Gilbert were still playing video games in the entertainment room when I got back to the house. Hamilton was elsewhere, probably tormenting more small furniture.

I nodded at the hack and slash game on the big screen. "That one of Hamilton's?" I asked.

"Naw," said the thin one—Gilbert? "All his games suck. We had to go into town and rent this one."

Three bags of chips and cheese puffs were open around them, and from the empties it looked like they had put away a case of some generic yellow soda between them—all before lunch. I guessed they hadn't picked up the food and drinks when they were in town, and a quick glance inside the empty snack cabinet proved it. I had no idea why they were here, but they were certainly enjoying the moment. I grabbed a bottle from the fridge and popped the top.

"That a beer?" the big one asked me.

"Root beer," I told him.

"Dude," he said, with what I think was supposed to be a laugh. "Is that like a training bra for real beer?" His friend sniggered.

"You're the one who's gonna to need a training bra. That stuff you're drinking shrinks your balls and gives you man boobs."

The thin one—Roscoe?—eyed his soda warily, and I left them to dwell on that cautionary nugget while I went to my bedroom to check my voice mail. The phone was one of those modern numbers made to look old-fashioney, with the push buttons arranged in a circle to look like a rotary phone. It made me want to stick my pinky finger out straight as I held it, like I was talking and drinking tea at the same time.

The phone at my ear, my finger poised over the dial, I felt someone's eyes on me and glanced up. It was Roscoe—or Gilbert—standing in the doorway and shaking his head at me.

"Dude," he said. He moved on.

I dialed my cell phone number and punched in my access code when the machine answered. An oddly soothing cross between a British woman and a Speak & Spell told me I had fifteen messages, and I closed my eyes and sighed. I had to go through with it, though. If I didn't do this now, there'd be twice as many tomorrow.

"Horatio, where are you? Mom says you're in Denmark—is that right? When did you apply for the foreign exchange program? Anyway, if you're going to be back anytime soon, there's this really cute intern here at the paper from James Agee High School. I think you guys would hit it off." Coming from my sister Desdemona, who has absolutely no luck with men, I somehow doubted she'd stumbled onto my soul mate. "Call me when you get back!" she told me.

Delete.

"'What a piece of work is man!'" My mom. The English lit. professor. "'How noble in reason. How infinite in faculty. In form and moving, how express and admirable. In action, how like an angel, in apprehension, how like a god.' And yet you can't be bothered to call your mother when you get to Hamilton's house? I will assume you are bleeding to death on the roadside in a twisted hulk of metal until you phone."

Delete.

"Hey, Horatio. It's Juliet. I'm showing my work at a student gallery on campus. Where are you? The opening's tomorrow night. Lots of hip, artsy college girls will be here, and they really go for that noble sarcasm thing you've got going—"

Delete.

"Pujols was two for four, with a double and a three-run home run. Just reached down and stroked into the left-center bleachers. A thing of beauty." Dad. Where I inherited my baseball gene. "Do you get Cardinals games where you are? Holland, or wherever? One of the other fantasy baseball owners offered a trade I want to run by you. Call me."

Save.

"Horatio, it's Desdemona again—"

Delete.

All in all, I got by with just six of my eight other family members calling me, which was low. Most of them thought I was in Europe somewhere, but even there they would have tracked me down eventually. I cleared the rest of the messages, then called Dad to get a brief baseball update and swear him to secrecy. After that I returned the receiver to its cradle with delicate yet refined grace and slumped my way back toward the entertainment room.

Hamilton had chosen to put in an appearance. He sat on the floor with his back to the couch where Roscoe and Gilbert were sitting. He was taking on one of them—Roscoe?—in Madden Football, and playing all kinds of sloppy, which was my first clue that something was wrong. Hamilton never lost at that game. I took a seat in the back row, sipped my unmanly root beer, and watched. Hamilton scrolled through the playbook with one hand while he took a sip directly from a bottle of vodka. He played another down, getting his player so turned around he started running toward the wrong end zone for a few seconds, which greatly amused Roscoe and Gilbert.

"Dude, you are so blitzed!" one of them said, laughing. Hamilton took another swig.

"So what have you guys been up to?" Hamilton asked, his eyes still on the screen. "I haven't seen you in, like . . . forever."

The fat one shrugged. "Same as always, I guess. Hang out. Watch TV. Shoot pool."

"What are you gonna do when you graduate?"

For the sake of my sanity, I assigned each of them names. "I think I might drop out. Get my PhD," said the one I called Roscoe. I tried not to weep for my generation.

"I think you mean 'GED,'" Hamilton told him.

"Whatever."

"I don't know," Gilbert said with a shrug. "We'll probably work at the plant like everybody else." He glanced behind Hamilton's head at his buddy, and then said to Hamilton, "Guess we don't have to ask what you're gonna do."

Hamilton took another drink from his bottle. "You mean you know all about my plans to go to Harvard and become a brain surgeon?" he said, starting to slur his words a little.

The boys laughed. "Right," said Gilbert. "Like you even need to go to college."

"You don't think I should?"

"Why would you?" Roscoe asked. He sipped off a two-liter of yellow-green soda. "You could graduate from high school and walk right into running the plant."

Hamilton focused intently on running in the right direction for a few seconds, and I started turning things over in my head. For a couple of slacker rubes, Roscoe and Gilbert suddenly seemed to be pretty focused. But just where were they going with this?

"Who says I want to run Elsinore Paper?" Hamilton asked, getting tackled.

He couldn't see it, but his question got him two very skeptical looks from the boys on the couch.

"Dude, how could you *not* want to?" asked Roscoe.

Hamilton went for it on an impossible fourth down where he should have punted. "How would *you* like it if somebody had been telling you since you were five what you were gonna do for the rest of your life?" Hamilton's QB got stuffed, and he turned the ball over on downs.

"See, that's just because you're not in *charge,*" Gilbert said. "You become the president of the company, you can fly anywhere you want in the company jet, do whatever you want. You'd be rich."

Roscoe grinned. "Filthy stinking rich."

Stinking is right, I thought.

"Ahh, I don't know," Hamilton told them.

"See, we know that's why you been moping around here," said Gilbert.

"You got ambition. Prospects."

"If only your uncle Claude hadn't gotten in the way."

They had been building up to this about as subtly as a blitzing linebacker. Roscoe threw a touchdown, and he and Gilbert did a knuckle tap over Hamilton's head.

"So, what," Hamilton said as they lined up for the extra point. "You think I should just kill Uncle Claude, get him out of the way?"

Roscoe missed the extra point by a mile, and he and Gilbert stared at Hamilton slack-jawed.

"I'm just kidding," Hamilton said, waving it away drunkenly. "That's just the booze talking, I guess. Here." He handed the other controller to Gilbert. "You guys finish it up. I gotta . . . I gotta go talk to Ralph on the ceramic phone," he said, clutching his stomach.

Gilbert made an effort to laugh, but he was clearly shaken. Roscoe too. Hamilton struggled to rise, then swerved toward the door. He saw me sitting there as he left, but he didn't say a word. I let him get a few steps down the hall, then got up and followed him. He was headed toward his room.

"That was a nice performance back there," I called out to him. He stopped in his doorway, then leaned on the door frame like he couldn't stand up. He staggered into his room without turning around and collapsed face-first on his bed. So that was how he wanted to play it. I pulled the bottle from his hands.

"Mind if I take a hit off your vodka?" I asked.

Hamilton knew I didn't drink, but he heard me take a long drink from his bottle. He sat up and frowned at me, as sober as a cold shower.

"Okay, there is no way you could know that was water and not vodka," he told me. I tossed the bottle back to him and went and closed the door so Beavis and Butthead wouldn't go looking for a bathroom and overhear us. Hamilton sniffed the bottle, trying to figure out how I knew.

"For one thing," I told him, sitting across from him in his desk chair, "I've seen you play Madden when you're drunk, and you're not *that* bad. For another, you never slur your words when you drink—you just eventually stop talking. And if you had really had as much vodka as I saw you drink just now, you wouldn't have wandered back to your room to pass out. You'd have just fallen asleep where you were. Plus, you usually never drink vodka—"

"All right, all right. Enough, detective."

"You weren't drunk this morning when you went nuts either, were you."

"No." Hamilton scootched back on his bed and put the vodka bottle with the water in it on his bedside table. "But I was mad."

"Yes, I think your unprovoked assault on the end tables was proof enough of that."

Hamilton put his head in his hands. "I—I'm sorry, Horatio. This whole thing has got me so turned around. One minute I'm furious and ready to fight, and the next I'm so depressed I can't see straight."

And in both cases, the drinking made it worse.

"So why the act with Roscoe and Gilbert?"

"Come on, Horatio. What are they doing here? I mean, seriously. I haven't seen either one of them for two years, and then suddenly they show up at my house and move into the guest bedrooms? Something's up with that, and since everybody thinks I walk around here drunk all the time anyway, I thought I could use that, maybe put them off their guard. But what was all that business about Claude and ambition?"

I picked up a baseball from Hamilton's desk and started flipping it toward the ceiling while I thought.

"Let's try it like this," I told him. "Hamilton comes home from school, and suddenly he's unhappy. He drinks. He doesn't enjoy sitting around doing nothing and playing video games like he used to. He attacks innocent furniture. 'What can be wrong with him?' his recently remarried mother asks. 'Heavens to Mergatroid,' his uncle and new stepfather says, 'who can tell with these troublesome teens? I have it—let's call in a couple of his former middle school chums.'"

"No way," Hamilton said, but he was turning it over.

"Look at where they went. As soon as they got an opening, they went right for the reason you've gotten all moody."

"And they seriously think I'm pissed off because Claude got in the way of my big plan to run Elsinore and get rich?"

I shrugged. "I admit it shows a serious lack of imagination, but . . ." I left the obviousness of that one unsaid.

Hamilton agreed.

"In the future, though, I think you should keep the cracks about killing Claude to yourself," I told him.

"Oh, come on. That was so obviously a joke."

"Obvious to you, maybe, but to two guys who honestly believe you're mad because Claude stands between you and joy rides on a Learjet?"

"Okay, so they think I want to kill Claude."

I caught the baseball and leaned forward. "Hamilton, if they're reporting back to Claude, and they believe you want to kill him—"

Hamilton blinked. "But he couldn't—I mean, he wouldn't honestly believe—"

"If you're right, and Claude is a killer—and I'm not saying you're right, but just suppose he is—don't you think that dropping hints about it and smashing up furniture and asking Roscoe and Gilbert if you should just kill him are maybe a *bad* idea?"

Hamilton didn't say anything, but I could tell he was spooked. And he should have been.

"Whoever killed your dad is a *murderer,* which means they could do it again—which means that a little more subtlety is required here."

"So what can we do?"

"For starters, we can go to the police, like we should have done from the start."

"No," said Hamilton.

"Look, I don't know why you're being so stubborn about this—"

"*No.* You said you would help me, and you swore you wouldn't tell anyone else. If you can't do anything, I will."

"No, no." I sighed. "I'll think of something."

"Then think of something already."

I flipped the ball in the air, a little miffed. It wasn't like hitting the intercom and ordering up another drink for yourself. *Um, yeah, could you send up another bottle of whisky, and, uh, oh yeah, the name of whoever it was who killed my dad? Thanks ever so much.*

"So, you stopped by the Brown-Water Rafting Race but you didn't say hello," I said. "Have you become an environmentalist all of a sudden, or were you just there protecting Elsinore's business interests?"

Hamilton pursed his lips and looked away.

"She's still got a thing for you, you know," I told him.

Hamilton looked at his sheets. I thought he might actually talk about this, about why he kept pushing Olivia away when it was so obvious that they both still had feelings for each other, but then he frowned and got touchy again.

"I notice that hasn't kept you from hitting on her."

"I wasn't hitting on her."

"Oh? Are you an environmentalist all of a sudden, or just protecting Elsinore's business interests?"

I gave him that one and kept tossing the ball.

"The play," I said suddenly. I put a little too much English on the ball and it smacked the ceiling. I ducked out of the way as it came crashing down onto his desk, knocking his keyboard to the floor.

"Damn, Horatio! Watch what you're doing."

"The new play opening in the community theater Friday night," I said, ignoring him. "Everybody's going to be there, right?"

Hamilton put on his disinterested history class face. "Not if I can help it."

"You'll be there, and you've got to help me make sure everybody else is too. Claude, your mother, Roscoe and Gilbert, Paul Mendelsohn, Ford Branff. And Olivia." We shared a look. "I can—I can ask her, if you want."

"What does Olivia have to do with all this?"

"Maybe nothing, but we can't rule anybody out yet."

"You're nuts," Hamilton told me.

"Just make sure everybody's going to be there," I said, reenergized. It was a crazy idea, but it just might work.

"What's the play?"

"Rosencrantz and Guildenstern Are Dead."

"Sounds boring."

"Don't worry," I told him. "If you get everybody there, you can go to sleep until the last act."

"Why? What happens in the last act?"

"That's when we find out who killed your father."

CHAPTER TWELVE

Night swimming is underrated, despite R.E.M.'s best efforts at promotion. Of all the amenities at Casa de Prince, the one I like the best is the Olympic-sized pool and outdoor Jacuzzi. The heir to the Prince fortune sat on a lounge chair while I made like a merman in the pool, the soft shimmering of the underwater lights the only illumination besides the stars. Hamilton was the real swimmer—he'd gone to the state finals both years he'd been on the varsity—but right now the only thing he was swimming in was a bottle. For real this time.

I emerged near Hamilton and held the side of the pool. "Who've you got so far?"

"For the play, you mean? Mom and Claude are going to be there, of course. I had one of the servants get in touch with Ford Branff, and he said he'd be there. Probably looking for another excuse to see my mother again."

"Or push his takeover bid."

"Same thing," Hamilton said. He swirled what was left of his drink and downed it. "Haven't talked to Paul Mendelsohn yet, but he'll do whatever Claude and Trudy tell him to do."

That left Roscoe and Gilbert and Olivia. There was still time to talk to all three.

Hamilton went for a refill from the bottle at his side but found it empty. He pressed a button on a side table, and a ghostly voice answered from an intercom on the wall behind him.

"*Sí*, Mr. Hamilton?"

"Another bottle of Jack Daniel's by the pool. We're out."

"*Sí, señor.* Anything else?"

"You want anything?" he asked me. I shook my head. "That's it."

"*Un momento,*" the voice promised, and the intercom went silent.

"It's so much easier to be a lush when they bring it to you, isn't it?" I asked him.

"Why are you riding me so bad about that lately?"

"Maybe I should have been riding you about it all along."

"Yeah, well, maybe it's getting on my nerves."

Hamilton was right—I had always stood by quietly and let him do whatever he wanted as long as he wasn't hurting anybody else. He was a big boy, and I figured he could take care of himself. I guess now I was beginning to think he couldn't.

Someone wearing bright red cowboy boots came out onto the patio, and I didn't have to look up to know it was Candy. Hamilton took a new bottle of whisky off Candy's tray without saying thanks and poured a new glass extra-slow and lovingly for my benefit. I wiped something out of my eye with my middle finger.

There was something else on the tray too, and Candy set it on the table.

"I took the liberty of bringing some warm milk, *señor,* for your friend the Boy Scout."

Hamilton stared at Candy, absolutely speechless. Thankfully, that rarely happens to me.

"I appreciate that, Candy," I told him. "In fact, find me when you get off work tonight, and I'll be sure to give you a tip."

"Ooh," he said, twisting my threat. "No thanks, big boy. I already have a date tonight." He whipped the metal tray up under his arm, turned on his high heel, and sauntered back to the kitchen.

"What—the—*hell*," Hamilton said. He sat up. "Do you two know each other or something?"

"Yeah," I told him. "We both used to ride for the Pony Express."

"How long have you been here, Horatio—three days? And you've already managed to piss off every last person in the house?"

"I only piss off people who deserve it," I said. "Hamilton, what do you know about that guy, anyway?"

"Who, that servant?"

"His name's Candy."

Hamilton shrugged. "He's just some Mexican. I don't know."

"There is something *very* weird about that guy. I mean, besides the cowboy getup."

Hamilton sighed theatrically. "I try not to bother about the lives of the little people."

I knew he was kidding, but in a way it was true. Hamilton pushed buttons and ordered drinks and waited for his car to be brought, and probably didn't give a second thought to who was doing the work for him. Mrs. Prince was probably the only Prince who knew their names.

"Yeah, well," I said, still a little pissy, "maybe if you drink enough, *everything* will stop bothering you."

"That's the idea. Either that or kill myself," he added. He suddenly got serious. "I've thought about it, you know. Killing myself."

"That's the stupidest thing I've ever heard," I said. I pulled myself up to sit on the edge. "If you're fishing for sympathy, you're going to need new bait."

"I'm serious," Hamilton said, staring up into the sky. "I mean, why not? At least then you get to sleep forever." He closed his eyes and kept his head tilted back, like he was communing with the stars or something. One of the few benefits to living in the middle of nowhere was a dark, clear night sky. It still smelled terrible, but it was pretty.

Hamilton opened his eyes and stared at his drink. "Then again, that might mean you dream forever too." He took a sip. "And who knows what we dream about when we're dead."

"We don't dream about anything," I told him. "We're food for worms. Suicide throws away the only miraculous thing you're ever going to see."

"Ah, but 'there are more things in heaven and earth, Horatio, than are dreamt of in your philosophy.'"

I flicked water on him. "Thanks. Because I've never heard that one before."

He grinned. "Anyway, you're right. And in the meantime, the only escape is to sleep—or drink."

"I hate sleeping," I said.

Hamilton laughed. "Of course you do!"

"What's that supposed to mean?"

He leaned forward and pointed at me with his glass. "You can't stand it when you're not calling the shots, when you can't see everything and hear everything and do everything. It's the same reason you don't drink. You never want to lose control."

"I don't see what's wrong with that," I told him.

"Sometimes it's nice to let go once in a while, Horatio." Hamilton leaned back on his lounge chair. "To just kick back and hit cruise control."

"Once in a while has suddenly become *all* the time for you, Hamilton. And before you drink yourself too silly, remember there's the little matter of your dead dad to attend to first."

I was a little more blunt than I meant to be, but I was mad that Olivia and now Hamilton had peeled open the layers of my ego so easily. Seriously, did I have "Analyze Me" tattooed on my forehead or something?

I slid off into the water and did a couple more laps, really pushing it hard. So I liked to be in control. How was that bad? How was not wanting to hand over the reins to someone else—or worse, to no one at all—a character flaw? I told myself that Hamilton was just another guilty drunk lashing out at someone with more willpower and stopped worrying about it.

As I got ready to do another lap I looked up and saw red painted toenails sticking out of a worn-out pair of Birks. I followed the frayed jeans up past nice hips and crossed arms to a familiar red baseball cap.

"Olivia," I said by way of hello.

"Aquaman."

"What?" Hamilton said, stirring. He hadn't seen her come around the pool from the house in the dark. "What's she doing here?"

"Hamilton wants to know why you're here," I said, even though we could all hcar each other just fine.

"Night fishing," she said.

"She says she's night fishing," I told Hamilton.

"I can hear her," he said.

I pulled myself up out of the water and stood dripping in front of her. I could see now she was carrying a paperback with a finger tucked in to mark her place, but I couldn't catch the title. She gave my half-naked body the once-over with her eyes and crossed to the chair next to Hamilton. She tossed me a towel and sat and opened her novel.

"Hel-*lo?*" said Hamilton. "What are you doing here?"

"Your uncle called my dad in for business stuff. I was with him in the car. So I came. End of mystery," she told him. Her eyes never left her book.

"No, what are you doing out *here*? With us."

"Seemed like a nice night for it. You know. Hanging out by the pool. I seem to remember a few nights sitting in this exact chair, as a matter of fact. And, come to think of it, you were in that one. When you weren't in this one with me."

Hamilton got up and moved a few paces away. "I don't know what you're doing here, but you can leave now."

"No thanks."

I didn't know what Olivia was playing at, but she was sure pushing Hamilton's buttons.

"Good night, Horatio," said Hamilton. He started to leave.

"Wait, I have something for you," Olivia called. Hamilton turned. He had a mean, calculating look in his eyes. I had seen that look before: right before he blew his perfect game and plunked the pitcher who hit me.

Olivia pulled a wad of rubber-banded envelopes out of her back pocket and tossed them on Hamilton's deck chair.

"One hundred and seventy-six poems, one for every day we were apart."

Hamilton got to know his drink better while he considered his response.

"I didn't write those."

"Oh, really? Like this one about that night we spent up on the bluff? Or the one that compares me to a mountain stream? Assuming of course you didn't mean the dirty Copenhagen River. Unless it was supposed to be a double entendre."

"I paid some loser kid in my English class to come up with that stuff."

"So, was it weird telling him all about the day we first kissed? 'Cause he kind of nailed that one."

They were putting on the kind of show where you want to get up and leave before intermission, but I wasn't really the audience. Olivia was walking the high wire for Hamilton, and I was her safety net in case he went crazy. I didn't like being used like that, especially against my friend, but she knew I wouldn't see her get hurt. Not physically, at least. From where I sat, she was angling for another kind of hurt—the kind I couldn't do anything about.

"Are you really this hard up?" Hamilton asked.

"What?"

"You're hot. You know, for a Denmark girl. Can't you find somebody else to fool around with in the backseat of a car?"

"You're a son of a bitch."

I definitely did not want to be here, but I stayed in case there were fireworks. Hamilton shrugged and had another drink. "You still have some good miles left in you. Something left in the tank a local boy could use. I only took you out on weekends and holidays, anyway."

"You bastard," Olivia said, standing. She was on the fence between outrage and sorrow, and she leaned toward sorrow. "You told me you loved me."

"I was just trying to get into your pants," Hamilton told her.

That was a lie, and I knew it. Olivia probably knew it too,

but sometimes your heart hears things differently than your head does—and always worse. She wasn't crying—I had to give her credit for that—but she had to work for it.

"I guess you really had me going then, because I thought we had something."

Hamilton walked up until he was in her face.

"Here's a piece of friendly advice then, Liv, since you can't seem to tell the difference. Any time a boy talks about your beautiful eyes, it's your breasts he's looking at. He writes you poems, he just wants to get laid. You're nothing but a piece of meat—a small-town country ham—and when he's had his fill, he'll move on to the next piece of ass and use the same old lines he used on you."

There was no stopping the tears now, and Olivia didn't try. They were the tears you only allow yourself in the darkness of a movie theater or huddled under your bedcovers or wherever it is you go when someone rips out our heart and stomps it flat on the ground. I don't know why she had come here, or what she thought she was doing, but she'd let Hamilton hurt her all over again.

"Better yet, you might as well give up men all together. No, come to think of it," he said, flinging the bits of ice and backwash from his empty drink into the pool, "women aren't any better. Maybe you should just be a nun."

Olivia brushed past Hamilton on her way out. I would have punched him or pushed him in the pool—and I think he actually *wanted* her to—but she didn't. She was a better person than me, that's for sure. I watched her disappear into the house.

"Gee, I forgot to ask her to come to the play tomorrow night," said Hamilton.

I got up. "You're a real piece of work, you know that?"

"Yeah. I'm a real bastard."

Hamilton hurled his glass with that pitcher's arm of his. It exploded on the wall underneath the intercom, scattering a thousand little shards into the water below. I could only imagine the team of scuba-clad maids they would need to clean that one up. He wanted me to lay into him for it, for everything, but I wasn't going to give him the satisfaction. I took a page from Olivia's book and walked away without a word.

The French doors to the back of the house were still open from where Olivia made her exit, and I slipped inside, careful not to get anything too wet. I wasn't in any hurry. I wasn't looking for Olivia, and I wouldn't have found her anyway. With those kind of tears, you don't just stop in the first bathroom you find. Besides, there wasn't a damn thing I could have said to make it any better.

Without my GPS tracker I got a little lost on my way back upstairs to my room. I went down an unfamiliar hall and heard the faint sound of voices coming from a room with the lights off. I figured it was a couple of the servants whispering sweet nothings to each other, or maybe plotting their revenge.

"I don't hear anything more."

"He might be asleep. He's had far too much to drink. Again."

It wasn't the help—it was Uncle Claude and Olivia's father, Paul. It sounded like they were talking about Hamilton, but how could they know what happened outside? I peeked inside and saw Claude flick a button on the intercom set in the far wall.

"Yes. Well. You see? I told you we'd learn something if we listened in." That was Paul, Olivia's father. "I think he's still in love with her. That's the reason he's been so melancholy lately. I suspect they're having a lovers' tiff."

I suspected that Paul Mendelsohn might be the only person left alive who still used the expression "lovers' tiff."

"I'm not so sure," said Claude.

"He's like a schoolboy, pulling the ponytail of a girl he likes. But I must say, he was yanking rather hard. Such language!"

"Whatever he's wound up about," Claude said, "I think he needs an *intervention*."

An "intervention"? What was that supposed to mean? I heard movement inside the room and slipped away before I could get caught snooping.

Besides, I had a hot date with Candy the Cowboy.

CHAPTER THIRTEEN

I sat in the dark thinking about Olivia and Hamilton as I waited for headlights to come around the bend. For all of his bluster, I had to agree with Olivia's father: There was still something between the two of them. Maybe they both still loved each other. But what made Hamilton want to hurt her so badly, and what made her keep coming back for more? And exactly what kind of "intervention" did Claude have in mind?

A car came down the gravel driveway, and I slid lower in my seat. I had gotten the Volvo without asking a valet to bring it around, then driven halfway down the Princes' long driveway. I was parked where the sweep of someone's headlights coming around the curve wouldn't catch me. Most of the servants went home earlier, right after dinner, but a few stayed until eleven o'clock to bring whisky and warm milk to people at the pool. Candy drove by in a beat-up little Mazda convertible with the top down. A bright orange ember glowed at the end of a cigarette bobbing in his mouth.

I waited until he was farther down the driveway, then pulled out with my lights off. The stars were still out, but the moon was just a sliver playing hide-and-seek in the trees. Candy pulled left onto the main road without signaling, and a few moments later I did the same. Olivia would have been so proud. Candy wasn't breaking any speed limits, though, and I was able to fall back a bit without losing him. His convertible crested a hill, and I flicked on my lights and became just another car going down the same lonely road through Denmark.

When Candy had mentioned that he was going to meet someone after work tonight, I figured this was as good a chance as any to learn something more about him. He was too strange, too odd a figure to be just another servant. He did everything he could to get noticed in a household that expected anonymity from its staff, and if Hamilton was any indication, Candy still managed to be invisible. Or maybe the Princes were all too wrapped up in their own problems to care.

We drove past the drive-thru and the supermarket and stopped at Denmark's only traffic light. This close, I could see that the Miata had North Carolina plates. Candy had a cell phone in his hand, and he was dialing a number up high on the steering wheel where he could still watch for the light to turn green. He put the phone to his ear, brought it back down to look at it, put it back to his ear, then flipped it closed and tossed it into his seat. The light turned green and he drove on through the intersection, leaving the last puff from his cigarette twirling around in little wisps for me to drive through. As far as I could tell, he hadn't made me yet, and I hung back again to give him some distance.

A little oasis of light emerged in the darkness up ahead, and I knew we were close to the interstate. I was debating just how far I would follow him when he turned off into the motel parking lot, again with no signal. I kept on going underneath the interstate, then pulled into a too-bright gas station and swung back out onto the road, heading toward the motel. There was a fast-food restaurant across the street that had already closed for the night, and I pulled into its empty parking lot, giving the hamsters under the hood a break. Candy stood beside his Miata doing a James Dean impression. He finished his cigarette and flicked it to the ground, then made his way across the parking lot to the motel. The doors opened to the outside, and Candy seemed to know which one he wanted.

I got out of the car and ran across the road, staying out of the streetlights. I circled around Candy's Miata, taking a quick look inside as I ground out his still-burning cigarette. The backseat of the car was a mess. It was filled with empty cans of Tab and crumpled fast-food bags and wrappers from restaurants you could find in Denmark.

Candy stopped outside room number 112 and knocked.

I slid in between a couple of cars so that I could see who came to the door and quickly pulled out my phone. It was finally in range—two bars' worth—but I wasn't looking to make a call. Instead I punched up the camera utility and took aim at the door as Ford N. Branff opened it and said hello to Candy the Cowboy.

Somehow I guessed he wasn't there to bring Branff another gimlet.

"Smile for the camera, boys," I whispered, and snapped a picture. My camera flashed.

Damn it, the flash!

Branff was already closing the door and Candy was scanning the parking lot. I backed out between the cars and started to run. Candy's cowboy boots clomped across the pavement behind me. I headed up a slope into some brush, and my arms took a thrashing as I scrambled as far back as I could. Almost blind in the darkness, I ran full tilt into a chain-link fence and spun to the ground, making slightly less noise than a change machine on a trampoline.

"Come out, come out, wherever you are . . ." Candy called. I could make out his silhouette as he patrolled the edge of the brambles. He was only a few feet away from me, and we both knew I couldn't hide there all night. He chuckled, then made what I took to be a tactical error and jogged back down the hill. I took another lashing as I worked my way back out of the brush, then ran for a large drainage ditch between the motel and the fireworks outlet next door. In my peripheral vision, I saw Candy lean into his car to get something—a flashlight?—then start to walk back in my direction.

He didn't look like he was in a hurry, but I was. I slid into the ravine and scraped the hell out of my hands, but it was dark here in between the pools of parking lot lights, and with any luck he still hadn't seen who I was. I jumped to the bottom of the gulley with a splash—why did there have to be water!?—and duck-walked into the mouth of a big metal storm drain. Spiderwebs clung to my hair and the trickle of water soaked my canvas shoes. Wonderful. This was shaping up to be a really terrific idea.

A few feet in I waddled around and watched through the gray hole, hoping nothing large enough to come up behind me and eat me called this drainage pipe home. Did bobcats live in this part of Tennessee? I was sure I had seen a television special about it.

Candy's shadow passed over the entrance to my little burrow, and I held my breath. There was a scuffling sound, a soft, quiet curse, and then nothing. Why didn't he just hop down into the gulley and shine his flashlight into the drain? I strained my ears. I heard an empty plastic bottle tumble farther down the ravine. He was looking for traces of me elsewhere, which meant he thought I might have already escaped into the night.

It felt like an hour passed. I don't wear a watch, and I certainly wasn't going to fool with my phone again to see what time it was. Was I actually going to get away with this after making such a stupid mistake? Then again, Candy might just be sitting on top of the concrete embankment that framed the storm drain, waiting for my legs to give out. But I had squatted behind a plate for more innings than I could count in the past three seasons, and I wasn't going to give in too soon. The question was, could Candy be that patient?

Loosened rocks and dirt cascaded into the water near the entrance to my bunker and I got my answer. He wasn't gone after all. I weighed the merits of inching farther into the pipe and decided to stay put. If he had a flashlight, it wasn't going to matter how far back I crawled.

The dark silhouette of a cowboy boot came down toward the water, then jerked back. More rocks came loose as Candy repositioned himself, and the boot bobbed again without settling into the gulley.

"Mierda," he cursed under his breath. "Are you in there, you *maldito*?"

If he had to ask, I wasn't going to answer.

Candy muttered something I couldn't understand, then tried to maneuver himself so he could hang over the top and peer inside. He held on with one hand while the other dangled below. Light glinted on the thing he held in his hand, and I saw that it wasn't a flashlight after all.

It was a gun.

Candy lost his balance, and the gun clanged on the metal above me as he used both hands to catch himself. He cursed again, and a few minutes later he kicked an empty can into the gulley. I guessed he was giving up, but there was no way to tell, and I didn't want to pop out and see Candy's gun again.

I settled in for extra innings

When I was almost too tired to keep my eyes open, I gave in. My knees popped and my calves clenched up as I inched toward the entrance. I straightened up when I could, but my legs still worked like I was wearing clown shoes. I looked around to see if Candy was sitting close by with a gun trained on me, then I relaxed. No one was there. All I could hear was the occasional semi blowing by on the interstate beyond the motel.

I scrambled up out of the ravine and made for my car across the street. Casting a glance back over my shoulder, I saw that Candy's Miata was still parked at the motel. Either Candy had a lot of information to report to his boss, or it was a sleepover. Maybe it was both.

The street was empty, and I hurried across it. I did a quick check of my car to see if Candy had found it and knifed the tires, now imagining him to be every kind of hood in every kind of gangster movie I had ever seen. The Volvo looked to be in good working order, though, and I slipped behind the wheel and drove away with one eye on the rearview mirror. I didn't even use my turn signal.

Closer to Denmark, when I was sure nobody was behind me, I flipped open my cell phone. That was going to be a long, wet, *painful* night for nothing if I'd managed to mess up the picture. I smiled. There on my phone were Candy the Cowboy and Ford N. Branff, together at the motel by the interstate.

Funny thing was, I think the flash actually helped.

CHAPTER FOURTEEN

I slept long and hard, and woke up feeling like a map that had been refolded wrong and stuffed in the glove box. My legs were pretty angry about my squat-fest the night before, and they let me hear about it. I stayed in the shower an extra ten minutes, and that seemed to help. I had a few scrapes and bruises too, but not so much as anybody would really notice.

Before I went downstairs in search of food and answers, I took one more look at the picture on my camera phone. I wasn't sure what to do with it yet. Candy and Branff were in bed together—figuratively and maybe literally—and that meant Branff's takeover attempt might have been more hostile than he wanted people to know. I made a note in my mental PDA: Candy the Cowboy and I were going to have to have a chat sometime soon.

I had finally memorized a path to the kitchen. It may not have been the shortest path, but I wasn't about to mess with something that worked. On the way, a door to one of the guest rooms opened and I stood face-to-face with Candy himself. This morning he was wearing brown denim pants and a shiny red cowboy shirt with white trim, which was partially obscured by the stack of pillows and sheets he carried. I wanted to ask him if there was a matching red cowboy hat somewhere, but the real question was whether he knew I was the parking lot paparazzi he had chased around a ditch with a gun. I waited to see what he would do.

"Well?" Candy said finally. "Are we just going stand here and stare at each other until one of us passes out from your cologne?"

So he didn't know it was me last night, after all. I grinned and I stepped aside.

"Say hello to Tonto for me," I told him as he passed.

The master of the house must not have ordered anything right then, because there wasn't anybody in the kitchen when I got there. I shook my head. The one time I wanted there to be somebody around, and I had the place to myself. That's the problem with servants—whenever you need one to make you a sandwich, they're off doing your laundry.

There was a bell—not a real one, but a button—but I couldn't bring myself to push it. It felt too much like whistling for a waiter. Instead I did the only other thing I could think of to bring a servant running: I started to help myself.

I banged around in the cabinets until I found a loaf of bread, and I had just stumbled on every kind of mustard there is except Colonel Mustard when a maid came hurrying into the room. She was squat and round and middle-aged and looked Mexican.

"I make you something?"

"*Gracias,* no," I told her. "I'm really not hungry. Ah, *no tengo hambre.*"

She looked at me strangely. "Then why you make sandwich?"

I liked her already. "I really wanted to ask some questions. Is that all right?"

She frowned, but apparently couldn't think of a reason not to. "*Sí*. All right."

"*Me llamo* Horatio," I said, finally putting my three years of high school Spanish to some kind of use. *"Como se llama?"*

"Catalina."

"Catalina, when Mr. Prince was alive—Hamilton's father—did you make all his food for him?"

"Ah, no. Sometimes, but others make food for him too."

"Other staff? Ah, *sirvientes*?"

"Sí."

"Nobody else cooked for him? His wife? Claude?"

She smiled, like I was being funny. "No."

"So all the food he ate went right from the kitchen to the table?"

Catalina kicked that one around. *"Sí,"* she decided.

Of course there was always room for an exception here or there, but Hamilton's father had said on the video that he had been poisoned little by little, over time. That meant someone had to have regular access to something he was eating or drinking.

"What about alcohol. Um . . . *cervezas*. Did he drink much?"

"Not *cervezas*. *Licor*."

"Liquor? Like tequila?"

"Johnnie Walker Black Label. Neat."

"Ah, right," I said with an embarrassed grin. The trouble with trying to talk to somebody in a language you barely know is that you come off sounding like a child, or worse, like a condescending American who had to take Spanish to graduate. I blushed, but her smile told me she was amused, not offended, by the effort.

"He drink as much as his son does now?"

Catalina looked sad at that. "No. Almost, but Mr. Hamilton drink too much these days."

"*Sí*. I'm with you on that one. Did he drink alone? By himself?"

"Mostly. *Sí*. But Mr. Claude drank with him."

"Often? *Muchas veces?*"

"*Sí*. Every Friday night." She hesitated. *"Mucho entoxicado."*

Entoxicado wasn't on any vocab list I had memorized, but I could guess it meant drunk. Very drunk. I nodded. "Every Friday?"

"*Sí*. Candy would tell us stories."

"Candy? As in Candy the gaucho?"

Catalina laughed behind her hand. *"Sí,"* she said. "He always volunteers to stay late, serve Mr. Prince and his brother."

Of course he did.

"Muchas gracias, Catalina. You've been very helpful."

"De nada, Mr. Horatio."

"Just Horatio. Thanks."

Catalina left me alone with my thoughts, and I got busy. It turns out I wanted that sandwich after all.

It was unexpectedly quiet when I went back upstairs. Hamilton wasn't in his room, and the Wonder Twins had vacated the entertainment room. I stood for a while, debated playing a baseball game on the big screen, then thought I'd go back to my room and try to sort things out instead. I had promised Hamilton results tonight, and I wanted to make sure I could get some.

There was a pile of clean sheets on my bed when I got to my room, which should have been my first clue that something was up. You never saw the work being done around here, just the end result, like little house elves came while you were gone and made everything in your room right again. I was stupid. I should have expected what happened next, but instead I walked right into it like some freshman poindexter strolling into the senior hall bathroom.

Candy whipped the door closed from where he hid behind it and sucker punched me in the side. It hurt worse than getting hit by a pitch, and I doubled over.

"Tonto sends his regards, jackass," said Candy. For some reason, the Mexican accent was completely gone, but I wasn't in much condition to ask him about that right then. He held me up to hit me in the same place again, and I dropped to my knees. He kicked me in the small of my back with one of those hard red cowboy boots, and I buried my face in the carpet and tried to keep my sandwich down.

"Can't the farmer and the cowman be friends?" I said with effort.

I expected another kick, but instead Candy pushed me over on my side and fished my cell phone out of my pocket. He sat down in an upholstered chair by the door while I coughed and sputtered on the floor.

"Don't get blood on the carpet," he told me, again without any accent. I felt like spitting up a great big phlegm-ball of blood and snot just for spite, but it seemed like an awfully uncomfortable way to get back at him. I watched as he opened my cell phone, clicked his way through a few menus, then deleted the picture I had taken last night. When he was finished, he flipped the phone closed and tossed it on the bed behind me.

"Nineteen new messages," he said. "You must be popular."

I pulled myself up straight using the corner of the bed.

"My family," I told him. "First time I've been in range all week was when I followed you to that motel."

Candy nodded and lit a cigarette. "Reception out here is a bitch."

"Remind me to complain about the room service too," I said.

Candy laughed. It was the first genuine laugh I'd heard all week.

"I like you, kid. A lot of the staff do. You're different from the jerks who live here, and they know it." He blew a puff of smoke at the ceiling. "They also know you're trying to figure out who killed Mr. Prince. They know just about everything that goes on in this house."

I worked myself the rest of the way onto the corner of the bed, and Candy didn't stop me. I tested my stomach. It felt like I'd slammed it in a car door.

"Do they know who killed him?" I asked.

Candy shook his head. "Neither do I."

"Sure you don't."

"Come on. Use your brain for something besides smart-ass comebacks," he said. "Okay, yeah, I've been spying on the Princes so Ford could get a little leverage in his takeover bid. But that's *all* I've been doing."

I tried to straighten my back, which opened up whole new worlds of pain.

"Like all that business Branff knew about Elsinore losing market share," I said.

"See? Isn't Candy good at his job?"

I grunted. "Branff must be paying you pretty well to play servant out here in the middle of nowhere."

Candy shrugged. "He's paying me, but it's . . . a personal favor too. The thing you need to understand is, I didn't have anything to do with Mr. Prince's death. And neither did Ford. All he's interested in is the paper plant."

"And Mrs. Prince."

Candy laughed. "He's not interested in Trudy." He crossed his legs and took another drag on his cigarette. "Trust me on that one," he said.

"So why not kill Rex Prince? Doesn't that get him one step closer to owning the place?"

Candy made a *tsk*ing sound. "Haven't you seen the way Claude acts? He's just as much in love with this stinking place as his dead brother was. This is his dream come true. He's finally king of the castle, and he doesn't want to sell any more than his brother did."

Candy was talking sense, but I generally didn't like to agree with people who had just beaten the snot out of me.

"You know, we could have had this conversation last night except you didn't want to get your fancy boots wet," I told him.

"But isn't this so much more comfortable?"

I tried to find some way to sit that didn't hurt. "Says you," I told him. "So now that your job's done, are you going back to Charlotte?"

All I had done was add Candy's North Carolina license plate to his connection to Branff, but his impressed look told me my math was right.

"If there *is* a God. My little tour of duty in this hellhole was almost over, and then Rex Prince up and died," said Candy. "Ford made me stay on to find out whatever I could, but I don't know what more there is to find out. Besides, I start rehearsals for *Don Quixote* at Actor's Theatre next month."

I nodded, finally understanding. "The accent."

"Method acting, *señor*."

"What about the getup?"

Candy looked hurt. "Well, I *am* roughing it out here." He stood to leave.

"So if you didn't kill Rex Prince," I asked him, "who did?"

Candy smiled, pushed a last burst of smoke out the side of his mouth, and stubbed his cigarette out on the back of the chair.

"If I knew that, sport, that information would be for Ford Branff's ears only."

"Which means you don't know."

Candy smiled again. "Anyway, sorry about the beatdown. I had to let you know that I can get to you whenever I want to, just in case you decided to tell your friend Hamilton about me and Branff."

"Message received," I told him. "But you should have known better too. I couldn't care less whether Elsinore Paper gets sold. I'm just looking for a killer."

"*Buena suerte* then, amigo," he said, slipping back into his role. "You're going to need it."

CHAPTER FIFTEEN

—💀—

I was a little surprised to see Candy's Miata in the parking lot of the Denmark Community Theater that afternoon. The play didn't start for another couple of hours, so the only people inside were the actors and stage crew preparing for their opening night performance. I kept an eye out for him and went inside the makeshift lobby. He had already said his piece, but my back and my ego were still bruised and I wasn't looking for an encore.

A middle school girl was working behind the ticket counter when I walked in. She had pigtails and a mouthful of braces that would set off airport metal detectors.

"Oh, hello! I'm sorry, the box office doesn't open for another hour," she said.

"I'm here to volunteer," I told her. "Mrs. Prince told me you needed someone to hand out programs."

"Great!" she said, a little too perky for my tastes. "What's your name?"

"Horatio. Horatio Wilkes."

"Hey! There's a character named Horatio in this play!"

"No kidding."

"Yeah, he's only a minor character, though."

I tried to smile. She consulted a list and frowned. "Well, I don't see your name on the volunteer list, and we already have someone coming in to do programs . . ."

"You know how it goes. People never show up for volunteer work." I put on the charm. "Unless they really care about theater. You do any acting?"

She blushed. "Nothing here. Not yet. But I was Anna in *The King and I* at Denmark Middle."

"I'll bet you were a hit," I told her. I made like I was looking around. "So where are those programs?"

"Oh," she said, still a little too loyal to that list. "I don't know—"

"Its okay, Lynn," said a familiar voice behind me. Candy stood in the passageway to the theater, *GQ*-ing it against the doorframe. I wasn't happy that he'd snuck up behind me twice that day, although this time he wasn't delivering any messages with his fists. "Mrs. Prince sent him here," he told the girl. "He's okay."

Lynn blushed again, but this time she was swooning. Candy had done with a lean what I couldn't do with words. Not that I wasn't grateful, but I wondered why Candy had helped me at all. Maybe he wanted to see where I was going with this, or maybe he was just feeling guilty over damaging my liver. Whatever the reason, I told him thanks and the girl with the braces went into the back to get the programs. Candy dropped the accent again while she was gone.

"I didn't expect to see you here," he told me.

"And imagine running into you in a theater," I said.

He shrugged. "Figured it couldn't hurt to stay sharp, pad the resume. It's a two-bit production, but what the hell—I was already here, and God knows there's nothing else to do in this town. It's a juicy part too—I'm the Player."

"I could have told you that."

Candy smiled. He looked me over, trying to figure out what I was up to with the programs but not seeing the angle. "Just remember what I told *you*."

"Parts of me remember very clearly."

Candy disappeared into the theater behind him as Lynn returned with a box full of staple-bound programs.

"It'll be a while before anybody gets here," she told me. "You can hang out in the greenroom with the actors if you want."

"I'll just grab a seat in the theater," I said. I had something to do, and the fewer people in on the gag the better.

Claude and Trudy Prince were the first suspects to arrive. While Lynn did a lot of fussing around over their tickets, Claude gave my presence by the door a wary look. He was starting to see enemies everywhere, and I couldn't blame him. Mrs. Prince thought it was wonderful—wonderful!— that I was so involved, and squeezed my arm to prove it. I told her Hamilton would be here soon and got another squeeze. I was shameless. I dealt them two programs off the bottom of the stack and considered the pair as they made their regal way to their reserved seats.

Claude was the easy answer to the puzzle. If becoming the CEO of a six-and-a-half-billion-dollar company wasn't motive enough, there was a lifetime of anger and resentment and envy to consider. What sweet revenge it would be to turn his brother's advice against him, to finally see something through to its completion, then slide into Rex Prince's job, his money, and his bed. And he had plenty of opportunity to poison Hamilton's father too, during those Friday night booze sessions.

Mrs. Prince hugged some friend from town, and waved to a few people who had already found seats in the back. She was the reigning queen of Denmark, to be sure—but she had been before her husband died as well. What did she stand to gain from Rex Prince's death? Loving her previous husband so much that she needed to marry his brother a couple months later was an odd way of explaining away the fact that she had jumped into bed with someone else pretty quickly. *Had* she and Claude been squeezing each other in private while Rex Prince was alive? Was his death one of passion, not finances? And while she may not have been cooking her husband's food, there were other ways to poison somebody. For all I knew, she'd been spiking his mouthwash with arsenic.

I shook my head. One week in Denmark and *I* was the one starting to see enemies everywhere.

A few people I had never met and therefore didn't suspect (yet) of killing Hamilton's father came in and got programs from the top of the stack. Then Ford N. Branff arrived. He did a double take when he recognized me. If Candy had known last night that I was the one snooping around the parking lot, Branff knew too. I gave him a smarmy smile. "Enjoy the show," I said, passing him a playbill from the bottom of my stack. He took the program warily and strode into the theater.

Ford Branff was harder to figure. I still didn't trust Candy's protests of his boss' innocence. Branff had a dangerous man on the inside, and could easily have ordered Rex Prince out of the way. And just because Claude didn't want to sell now didn't mean he and Candy had known that before. What if they had poisoned Hamilton's father, thinking Claude couldn't resist a six-billion-dollar carrot dangled in front of his nose? Or maybe they had bet on Branff's charm to sweet-talk Mrs. Prince into selling before Claude got tangled up in the mix. No matter what, the media mogul was used to getting what he wanted, and Rex Prince's death spelled opportunity of one kind or another.

Paul and Olivia Mendelsohn came next. Hamilton was right: What Claude and Trudy commanded, Paul obeyed, usually dragging his daughter along for the ride. Olivia wasn't in the mood to talk, much less look at me, and I couldn't help noticing she wasn't wearing my Cardinals cap. I wanted to say I was sorry—for everything—but I knew that wasn't anything she wanted to hear right now. Worse, I still suspected Olivia could have had something to do with the death of Hamilton's father, and I hated myself for even thinking it.

Olivia wanted the Copenhagen River to be clean, and she wanted the Prince family to pay for it. Rex Prince claimed it wasn't possible; Ford Branff told us it was. Maybe Olivia had decided the old man needed a taste of his own poison. She seemed to have the run of the Prince house whenever her dad was around, but it still didn't seem her style. It was easy to think that she might have wanted to punish Hamilton too— but I had to remember that Hamilton and Olivia hadn't broken up until *after* his father's death. If she *had* been involved in his father's death, she had certainly paid a larger price for it than she could ever have bargained for.

Pops Mendelsohn got a program from the top, and as much of a stretch as it was, Olivia got one from the bottom.

Hamilton was among the last of the audience to filter in, and I was surprised to see Roscoe and Gilbert tagging along. He had stayed clear of me all afternoon, maybe embarrassed by his little performance by the pool, or maybe not. He came over to see me while the boys bought their tickets.

"I can't believe you got them to come," I said.

"I had to tell them somebody got naked in the third act. What are you doing?"

"Handing out programs," I told him. I slid him one from the bottom of the stack.

"Yeah, I can see that. But I mean, what are you up to? How is coming to some dumb play going to prove anything?"

Roscoe and Gilbert walked up, and I put on a barker's smile.

"Here you go, gents. Programs. Programs."

"Hey," said the one I was calling Roscoe. "How come you gave me one from the bottom of the stack?"

I blinked. He was the first person who'd noticed.

I laughed. "Wha—I didn't even realize," I told him. "Here." I took his program and put it on the bottom, flipped the stack over so the bottom was the top, and gave the same program back to him. "There you go."

"Dude, Hamilton said somebody gets naked," said Gilbert. "Izzat true?"

"Very nearly," I told him.

"What, just down to pasties or something?"

The house lights dimmed a couple of times, and the audience grew quiet.

"In you go," I told them. "Hamilton, I saved us a couple of seats near the back."

When the lights went down I left the rest of the programs in a folding chair by the door and went inside to find my seat. Roscoe and Gilbert sat close by. Claude and Mrs. Prince were down front, Olivia and her father were in the risers on the other side of the theater, and Ford Branff was sitting midway up to our right. It had taken me a while to find just the right place in the theater where we could see everyone and, most importantly, the stage.

The director of the play came out, and it being opening night, took a while to give special thanks to the sponsors and volunteers who had made the magic happen.

Hamilton leaned over and whispered at me. "Okay, seriously, Horatio. What's going on?"

"Turn to page seven in your program," I told him.

Hamilton rolled his eyes and sighed. He flipped through the photocopied booklet until he found it: a full-page ad for Elsinore Paper, proud sponsors of the Denmark Players. There with a marker I had written, "I know what you did to Rex Prince. I have proof. Meet me behind the stage after the pirates attack."

"'After the pirates attack'? What is that supposed to mean, 'after the pirates attack'?"

"It means go backstage after the pirates attack. I don't know how much clearer it can be."

"Did everybody in the theater get one of these?"

I gave him a look that asked him just how stupid he thought I was. "No. Just the people who had a reason or an opportunity to kill your father."

"How do you know any of them are going to see this?"

"If there's one thing everybody does," I whispered, "it's read the program before a show. There's nothing else to do while you're waiting."

A few seats down, Roscoe and Gilbert had rolled up their programs and were using them to thwack each other.

"Well," I said, "almost nothing."

Unfortunately, the pirates didn't attack until act three. The play roughly followed the plot of Shakespeare's *Hamlet,* focusing on the minor characters of Rosencrantz and Guildenstern. Personally, I'm a little tired of every author without a bright idea of his own putting a modern spin on a "classic," but I was a big fan of *Rosencrantz and Guildenstern Are Dead.* Apparently Hamilton wasn't. He drove me nuts the whole play.

"Do the pirates attack soon?"

"No."

"Now?"

"No."

"Do the pirates attack any time this act?"

"No."

And so on.

When the third act finally arrived, Hamilton was on the edge of his seat. Candy, as the Player, got to do some of his best work in act three. He was using a different voice and carried himself in a completely different way, and I had to admit he was good. But that just meant he could have been acting innocent when he smoked a cigarette with me in my room.

"Hey, do I know that guy?" Hamilton asked.

"He's brought you a drink once or twice," I whispered back.

As the act wore on, Hamilton slumped in his chair. Then someone on stage yelled, "Pirates!" and suddenly people were running back and forth across the stage fighting and dying.

"This would be the pirate attack," I told Hamilton. "Now watch."

Instead of focusing on the melee happening on stage, we watched the audience. "Come on, come on," I muttered. "One of you get up."

Mrs. Prince stood.

"No," Hamilton whispered.

Hamilton was about to leave his seat. I put an arm across

his chest and looked around the room. Down to our right, Ford Branff was still in his seat, his eyes on the stage, but on the other side, Olivia was already gone. Damn, when was the last time I had looked for her?

"It can't be my mom," Hamilton said. I held up a finger to tell him to wait, then pointed it across the room. Mrs. Prince was just getting up so Claude could get past her, and she sat back down once he had gone.

"Claude," Hamilton said. "What are we waiting for? Don't we have to get backstage? Make sure he's not just getting up to go to the bathroom?"

"Patience, grasshopper." I directed his attention toward the stage.

The pirate attack had finished and the Player (Candy) and his troupe had retaken the stage to banter with Rosencrantz and Guildenstern. The play was almost over, and the Player was trying to tell them that it had to end with death. Their deaths. They were building up to the scene I had watched being rehearsed when I sat in the stands with Mrs. Prince the day before. The way the trick worked, the two hanged dummies would be magically revealed behind what stage techs call "scrim." It's a big piece of gauze that looks opaque until you shine light on the back. Then you can suddenly see whatever's behind it like you're looking through a window.

"Show!" cried the Player with a flourish.

The lights came up. The scrim disappeared. The bodies of Rosencrantz and Guildenstern appeared, swinging from ropes.

And right below them, illuminated for everyone to see, stood Claude Prince.

The audience cracked up. There probably wasn't a person there who didn't know him, and half of them probably worked for him. The actors on stage froze. Claude's face went from shocked to scared to embarrassed all in the span of about three seconds.

"Sorry," he joked, "just looking for the bathroom."

I didn't have to point out to Hamilton that the only bathroom in the place was in the lobby, and there was little chance that his stepfather could have gotten that turned around. The audience didn't seem to care, though, and they ate it up as Claude slinked away.

"Psst, hey!" Roscoe called back to us. "I like the pirate stuff and all, but when do we get to see some boobs?"

CHAPTER SIXTEEN

I sat in the kitchen the next morning waiting for my coffee to reach my toes. After the play I had stayed up until I was sure everyone else had gone to sleep—even Roscoe and Gilbert, who played video games until two a.m.—and then taken care of a little business that I hoped would pay off later. I wasn't sure if my hunch was right, but if I had waited, I might have missed my chance. Still, I was paying for it now.

A few of the Prince family's servants were busy cutting grapefruit and frying bacon and making toast, and I admired their abilities to function before noon. The hard drive in my brain was just starting to spin up, and the number one item on today's task list was Claude. Now that we knew he was our mark, how did we prove he killed Hamilton's father?

Candy came into the kitchen, there for work but apparently not yet on the clock. He saw me the moment he walked in. He poured himself a cup of coffee, grabbed a bagel, and sat down across from me at the little breakfast table in the corner. For a few minutes we pretended not to know each other, and then he started talking so just the two of us could hear.

"I suppose I have you to thank for ruining my best scene."

"Yeah, sorry about that," I told him. "You were good, though. Good stage presence."

"So, can I take it you know Claude Prince killed his brother?"

"If I did, sport, that information would be for Hamilton Prince's ears only."

Candy recognized his own words and saluted me with his bagel.

"So how do you plan to rein your boy in?"

"Hamilton?" I asked. "What do you mean?"

"I mean, how do you plan on keeping him from doing something stupid? Ford is very interested in seeing Claude go to jail—*if* he's the killer. Like I told you, all he cares about is the plant. Hamilton doesn't seem to want it, but he can't sell it to Ford if he's in jail."

"Are you talking about revenge? Hamilton wouldn't do anything that stupid."

Hamilton walked in just then, and I was surprised to see him awake so early. I was even more surprised to see what he was wearing. On top of jeans and a T-shirt he wore an eye-scalding orange hunting vest and an orange hat with earflaps. By ten thirty he'd be roasting.

Hamilton came over to the table where we sat. "We're going hunting," he said. "Want to come?"

Candy shot me an "I told you so" look, then watched Hamilton out the side of his eyes and drank his coffee with both hands.

"You mean you're actually going outside in that getup?" I asked.

"You should see Claude's gear. It's a bright orange camo print. In case he has to hide out in an orange grove."

There was something strange about Hamilton, like his

body was moving in slow motion. It was a subtle thing, but he seemed to really focus on the simple act of sitting down at the table.

"Is he going with you?" I asked. "Claude?"

Hamilton reached out and slowly took a Danish from a tray on the table. "Nope. It's just me and my mother."

I set down my coffee. "Hamilton, we haven't talked about last night. About your uncle." Candy was going to hear our whole conversation, but I didn't care and Hamilton probably didn't even think of him as a real person sitting with us.

"What is there to talk about?" he said. He was still supernaturally calm. "You saw the same thing I did."

"We haven't talked about what we're going to do now."

"Got any ideas?"

"No," I admitted. "But I haven't been working on it long enough to—"

"Orange juice," Hamilton said. "I think I want some orange juice."

I blinked as he got up from the table in mid-conversation to seek out a glass of OJ.

"He's drunk," Candy said quietly.

"What? He can't be. It's eight o'clock in the morning."

Candy shrugged. "If you say so. But Catalina told me she took him drinks all night long. He never drank so much that he passed out, just sat by his window looking out at the stars or something."

If Hamilton had some kind of buzz on, it was a new kind of drunk for him, one I couldn't anticipate. I closed my eyes and cursed myself. Why had I thought Hamilton would take the revelation about Claude lying down?

Hamilton returned with his glass of orange juice and drank it like it was nectar of the gods.

"Hamilton," I said. "Hamilton, are you listening to me? We can't do anything stupid now."

"Sure. Of course not," he said. "We'll just wait until you come up with something clever."

I narrowed my eyes. "You seem to be taking all this pretty lightly."

Hamilton stood. "Meet me in the mudroom if you want to go."

He left, and I closed my eyes and sighed. When I opened them again, Candy was smiling at me over his cup of coffee.

"Shut up," I told him as I stood to follow Hamilton. "Just shut up."

Hamilton had just finished lacing up his boots when I found him. He nodded when he saw me and pulled a bright orange vest off a peg.

"Here, put this on," he said. "It was my dad's."

"Is this really necessary?" I asked. I meant more than the orange vest.

Hamilton turned around with a rifle cradled in his arms—a .22 by the smallish looks of the bullets he was feeding into it. It was a squirrel-hunting gun, a small-game rifle kids learn to shoot with. He locked the bolt with a click.

"Safety first," he said. "You wouldn't want to get shot by accident now, would you?"

"Hamilton, wait." He went outside and I followed him like a lemming. "I don't think you've got a clear head. Let's go back inside. Play a video game or something."

"No, man. You've got it all wrong. I see everything clearly now. For like the first time ever."

I was pretty sure now that Hamilton planned on doing something completely idiotic, but there was no stopping him short of tackling him. Mrs. Prince waited for us on the lawn and we said our hellos. She frowned at Hamilton's gun.

"Do you really need to bring that?" she asked. "Why don't we just go for a walk instead?"

"Dad and I used to go hunting every Saturday morning. Or did you forget?"

"I haven't forgotten, Hamilton," she said tiredly. "Shall we go?"

Hamilton turned to me and smiled. "Come on. Claude said he might join us later."

So there it was. Mrs. Prince walked down the hill behind the house, where a well-worn path led to a thick forest of deciduous and pine. Hamilton was right behind her, and I brought up the rear. Call me paranoid, but I couldn't help feeling like I'd been brought along as a witness.

"Hamilton. Hamilton!" I called.

He stopped while his mother walked on ahead.

"What's going on here?"

"We're going for a walk in the woods."

"With a gun? Is it even legal to hunt anything right now? It's the middle of summer."

Hamilton shrugged. "I'm sure something's in season."

I caught his arm. "Hamilton. You're drunk. You may be hiding it, but I know."

"What if I am?" he asked.

"Oh, Hamilton. This is *so* not the time to do something stupid."

"Is there a right time to do something stupid?" he asked. "I tell you what. When that time comes, you let me know, okay?" He shook me off and headed down the trail again.

I could have stayed behind. I could have gone back to the kitchen and finished my breakfast and let Hamilton be responsible for himself for a change. What was I, anyway, his best friend or his babysitter?

I kicked at a root growing across the path. I was his best friend, damn it, and I followed him into the woods. Hamilton and his mom walked on ahead and I stayed close enough to listen in but far enough away so I wasn't part of the conversation.

"Hamilton, you've offended your stepfather," Mrs. Prince was telling him.

"Well, you've offended my *real* father."

"Why does everything you say these days have to be smart?"

"Would you rather I said something stupid?"

"I would rather you say nothing at all if you're going to be nasty," Mrs. Prince told him.

"And I wish you had said nothing when Claude asked you to marry him." Hamilton stopped. "I mean, what were you *thinking*?"

"I was thinking that I loved him, Hamilton."

"Don't—*don't*," he told her. "Say that you were lonely. Say that you needed a replacement husband or whatever you say to rationalize it. But do *not* say you're in love. Not with him. Not Claude."

Mrs. Prince's voice rose. "Why do you hate your uncle so much?"

"You don't know how much he hated Dad. How jealous he was. You don't know what he *did* to him, but I do."

"'What he did to him'?" Mrs. Prince repeated. "Does this have something to do with that ridiculous thing in the program last night? Did you write that?"

Whoops. I hadn't considered that everyone who didn't understand that message would want to know what it was all about.

"Claude wanted everything Dad had, couldn't you see that?" Hamilton said. "He wanted the paper plant. He wanted respect. He wanted *you*. But the only thing he ever did to earn any of that was to *kill my father*."

Mrs. Prince backed away. "Hamilton. Listen to yourself. Listen to what you're saying!"

"Are *you* listening? You married the man who killed your husband!"

Mrs. Prince turned and walked back past me toward the house, putting me quite literally in the middle. I pretended to study a twig on the ground.

"Don't walk away from me," Hamilton told her.

Mrs. Prince kept walking.

"I said don't walk away from me!" Hamilton yelled. It was barbaric and over the top and it made the hair on my arms stand up. I could see it had an effect on Mrs. Prince too. She froze, then slowly turned.

"Or what, Hamilton? Will you shoot me? Do you hate me that much?"

Faster than I could think to duck or yell, Hamilton whipped the rifle up to his shoulder and pulled the trigger. The air exploded. Mrs. Prince dropped to the ground.

"Hamilton, what the—" Then I saw somebody else behind Hamilton's mother, a man dressed in bright orange camouflage. He staggered like he'd been punched in the chest, then fell backward like a dead man.

Hamilton hadn't shot his mother, he'd shot Claude Prince.

Mrs. Prince crouched a few yards away, her hands on her head like she was practicing a tornado drill. Hamilton stood in shock, the gun still at his shoulder. I pushed the rifle down so it was aimed at the ground and rushed to Claude's side.

Only when I got there, I saw that it wasn't Claude Prince.

It was Paul Mendelsohn, the family lawyer. He was staring at the sky like he couldn't for all the world figure out why he was lying here in the forest on a damp Saturday morning. He was wearing what I guessed was Claude's hunting vest from Hamilton's description of it. It had been orange once, but a dark black-red stain was wicking its way out from his chest.

"Mr. Mendelsohn?" I asked. "Mr. Mendelsohn, can you hear me?"

"I just—I just came to get Mrs. Prince to sign some papers—" he muttered.

I saw now there was a wad of papers in his hand, and I took them from him and tossed them aside. I tore the vest open and saw where the blood was coming from, just north of his heart.

Apparently it was open season on lawyers.

I ripped my own vest off and pressed it into his wound, then fumbled my cell phone out of my pocket with one hand and flipped it open.

Out of area.

"Hamilton! Oh my God!" Mrs. Prince was crying behind me. "Hamilton, what have you done?"

"What have I done?" Hamilton asked. The question seemed to wake him up. "What have *I* done? Nothing worse than what he deserved! Nothing worse than murdering my father and marrying my mother!"

"Hamilton—" Mrs. Prince said, sobbing. "Oh, Hamilton."

"It isn't *Claude,* Hamilton," I yelled. "It's Olivia's father, and he needs a hospital. *Now.*"

Hamilton and his mother stared at me like I was speaking Martian.

"Mrs. Prince," I said, looking her right in the eyes. *"Get back to the house and call an ambulance."*

Her universal translator kicked in, and she finally comprehended what I was saying. She nodded frantically and ran back up the path toward the house, giving me and the family lawyer a wide berth. Paul had slipped into unconsciousness while I'd been barking at the Princes, and I cursed. The wadded-up vest I held against his chest was getting hot too. Hot, wet, and sticky. I tried to reposition it, but it didn't help.

There was no way around it. No matter what I did, I was going to have blood on my hands.

CHAPTER SEVENTEEN

— 💀 —

An ambulance finally came for Paul Mendelsohn, and a police cruiser came for Hamilton. Ordinarily, the family lawyer would have been able to help him out of a jam like this. The trouble was, Hamilton had just *shot* the family lawyer.

The initial news on Olivia's father was good—the bullet had shattered his shoulder blade but missed the things that made him tick. He'd be in the hospital for a while, but he'd live. It remained to be seen whether he'd press charges or not. He was still unconscious.

Hamilton was taken down to the station for questioning, then released. They asked me questions too, but I didn't have to get taken downtown for it. I told them what I saw, but with the mute button on: We took a walk in the woods, Hamilton thought he saw a squirrel or a wildebeest or a lion or something, and he shot it. It turned out to be his ex-girlfriend's dad.

Mrs. Prince was a mess, but Claude was there to console her just like always.

"It's my fault," he told her. "I sent Paul out there with those papers. If I hadn't—"

I wondered if Claude had dressed the family lawyer up

in his hunting vest and sent him to Hamilton on purpose, to test the waters. The thought gave me a shiver, which wasn't helped any by the calculating look on Claude's face when Mrs. Prince buried her face in his shirt. If Claude was willing to trade pawns in a chess match, who would be the next piece to fall?

After the fun of life support and police interrogation died down, the Prince house got quiet. I passed through it like a ghost, trying to decide who I was going to haunt next. I wanted to rattle the chains for Claude, but it would have to wait until things cooled down. Instead I went out by the pool, where Hamilton lay hiding behind his sunglasses. He looked pretty relaxed for having shot a man this morning, but I think the half-empty bottle of whisky by his side had a lot to do with that.

I sat down on the lounge chair beside him but didn't say a word. He knew I was there just the same.

"Don't," he told me. "Just . . . don't."

The French doors to the house banged open and Olivia Mendelsohn marched around the pool to where we sat. Her face was streaked with tears, and her fists were balled for action.

"Stand up," she told Hamilton.

He didn't budge.

"Stand up, you bastard!" she screamed.

Hamilton pulled himself up with extraordinary effort and stood in front of her. He swayed.

"Take off your sunglasses and look me in the eyes."

He did what she asked, dragging them slowly away from his face. His look was vacant, but somehow he trained his gaze on the girl in front of him.

I figured it would be a slap, but Olivia reared back and socked him a good one in the eye. He almost went down from the booze and the belt, but I was there to catch him—and hold him in case the alcohol made him forget he'd never hit a woman. Hamilton shrugged me off like he knew what I was doing and was insulted, but his head must have been ringing from that shot and he let me push him back down in his chair.

It hurts like hell when you hit a guy right, and Olivia held her hand like she'd broken it. She also wasn't complaining. She didn't say a word to me as she turned and stalked away, and I didn't expect her to.

Hamilton raised a hand to his already swelling eye and recoiled in pain.

"Sonuva bitch," he moaned.

There was an ice bucket on the table for Hamilton's drinks, and I put a couple of handfuls in a towel and offered it to him. Hamilton snatched it and winced as he put it to his face.

"So, you're there to catch me, but not stop her from punching me."

"I figure you had it coming."

Hamilton slid his sunglasses back on and tried to work the ice bag up under them.

"You're a strange kind of friend, Horatio."

"Yeah," I told him, "but don't forget that I am one. And you're running out of them."

Hamilton probably would have questioned my friendship further if he'd known where I went after I left him. I had promised him that I wouldn't tell a soul, that we would solve the puzzle of his father's murder without anyone else's help, but as far as I was concerned even a double-swear spit-shake deal was over when somebody got shot.

Denmark was a tiny town, and it wasn't terribly difficult to find the local cop house. I parked my off-white, off-cool Volvo in one of the parking places out front and went inside. It was a small building, just one room with a couple of little cubicles to one side. Wanted posters and public service announcements were tacked onto every free space on the wall, and there was a distinct smell of leather polish and chewing tobacco in the air. Two messy desks sat behind a long, high counter that separated the officers of the law from the common rabble like me, and the only policeman in the joint sat at one of them eating a sandwich and reading a newspaper.

The venetian blinds on the door announced my presence with a rattle and a slap.

"Help you?" the cop said. His accent was pretty thick, but luckily I'm fluent in both English and Appalachian.

"My name's Horatio Wilkes. I'm a friend of Hamilton Prince. Staying with him for a few weeks this summer."

"Gonna stay with him in jail too?" He snorted at his own joke.

"Has Mr. Mendelsohn pressed charges?"

"Naw, the shyster's too loyal. Woke up and told us it was just an accident. No charges. Unless you got something more to add . . ."

"No. Not about that. About a murder."

His eyebrows went up at that one.

"Murder?"

"Is there a detective I can talk to?"

The officer grinned like I was an idiot. "Oh, I think I can handle it. Let's see," he said, standing and patting his pockets. "Now, let me just find my detective's notebook." He grabbed his sandwich wrapper and smoothed it out on the counter that separated us.

"Here now. That oughta work." He clicked a ballpoint pen and grinned at me. "Now, who's been murdered?"

I hate adults who treat teenagers like we're still in grade school, but I needed this buffoon to listen to me so I swallowed it.

"Rex Prince. My friend Hamilton's dad."

He licked the pen and said "Rex Prince" as he wrote it. "The one who's already dead, you mean?"

"Already murdered. Yes."

"Doctors said that was cancer. Not likely to miss a thing like that, eh?"

"I think he was misdiagnosed. Was there an autopsy done?"

He laughed. "I think you've been watching too much TV, son. Tell me, how are you so sure he was murdered?"

"He said so. In a videotape he left for his son. He said someone was trying to kill him."

That got the guy serious for a second.

"You got this video with you?"

"No. But I can get it."

He nodded and leaned forward conspiratorially. "And uh, who do you suspect did it . . . Professor Plum, in the billiard room, with the rope?"

He had himself a good laugh at that one, and I learned he'd ordered onions on his sandwich.

"No," I told him. "I think it was Claude Prince, in the entertainment room, with the poison."

He stopped laughing real quick and wadded up the sandwich wrapper.

"That's a pretty serious charge, young man. Claude Prince is well-liked in this town. Especially down here at the station. He's a volunteer firefighter, member of the Fraternal Order. Hell, he's almost an honorary deputy."

I closed my eyes and cursed my own stupidity. Why hadn't

upstairs to the entertainment room, I found Roscoe and Gilbert camped out in front of the giant screen, as usual. No one else was in the room. They spared me a glance and went back to watching an old movie called *Strange Brew*. Panting a little from the dash, I crossed to the liquor cabinet and had a look. The bottle of Johnnie Walker Black Label—Hamilton's father's favorite drink—was gone. I laughed once mirthlessly under my breath and nodded. Then I had a moment's panic.

"Hey, you guys didn't drink the Johnnie Walker, did you?"

"Naw, man," said the thin one. "And we ain't seen nobody come in here and take it neither."

The fat one gave him a nudge.

I closed the cabinet. "Thanks for clearing that up."

Either Claude had gotten it sometime in the night, or he'd just burst in on Chang and Eng here and promised them *Ultimate Fighting Championship Twenty-six* on pay-per-view not to mention they'd seen him take it. It looked like my hunch was better than Quasimodo's.

I had to think. Roscoe and Gilbert were like a mental black hole, so I wandered down the hall to my room. I stopped short when I saw one of the hired help tidying my personal effects.

"Um, can I help you?"

"Excusa," the fellow said. "Just straightening up."

"Straightening up what?" I asked.

"The room, *señor*. It was a mess. Clothes and things all over the place."

I'm kind of anal about keeping my clothes folded and in drawers, not on the floor. Hamilton and Olivia would probably use that as exhibit Q in the case for me being a control freak, but there it is. Long story short, I didn't leave the room all messed up.

I remembered those honorary trophies in Claude's office? Of *course* Claude had the local police in his pocket. He'd never earned anything, but you give enough money and *anybody* will make you a member.

"You say there's a videotape?" the policeman asked me.

Yeah, I thought, but the only way you're gonna see it is on the six o'clock news. I needed an honest cop, and that might mean having to call my sister Miranda.

Before I could answer him, the door behind me clattered open and Claude Prince strolled into the office.

"Hello, Claude."

"Heya, Jimmy," Claude said. Great. He was on a first-name basis with the local constabulary. Smart, Horatio. Very smart.

"Just here to settle this mess with my son," said Claude. He turned to me. "Hello, Horatio. I'm surprised to see you here."

"He's here with some very interesting information," Officer Jimmy said.

"Actually, I was just leaving," I told them. "I'll tell your 'son' you were down here looking out for him."

I pushed past Claude before Jimmy could rat me out, but I was just delaying the inevitable. I slid behind the wheel and turned the key and the Volvo coughed to life. Inside, Jimmy was leaning over the counter, no doubt giving Claude the rundown on my accusation. He pointed in my direction, and Claude glanced over his shoulder and caught my eyes.

So he knew for sure now we were onto him. Fine.

I threw the car in reverse.

Game on.

CHAPTER EIGHTEEN

— 💀 —

I flew down the road to the plant and talked my way in through the gate. Hamilton's pals Frank and Bernard weren't on duty yet—they worked the late shift—so a different security guard met me at the little concrete bunker.

"You say Hamilton sent you down here for something he left? We ain't found nothing."

I walked inside the guardhouse like I'd been there a hundred times before.

"We were down here the other night saying hello to Frank and Bernard," I said, doing some blatant name-dropping. It seemed to work, and the guard relaxed a little. Inside the control room, another guard sat half watching the bank of television monitors scanning the plant grounds. He was surprised to see me walk in, but not so much that he could be bothered to get up.

"What's wrong?" he asked.

"I'm just looking for something Hamilton left the other night." I spied the coffee tin up on the shelf and hauled it down.

"Here we go. Thanks, guys."

The guy who greeted me outside stood in the doorway.

"Hamilton didn't leave that," he told me. "That thing's been there for ages."

"Long as I've been working here, easy," the other guard said. "Ain't nothing in it."

I gave the can a rattle, partially to prove to myself that what I wanted was still in there. It was.

"There is now," I told them. "Uh, listen guys," I said low, like we were pals sharing a secret. "Did I say Hamilton and I came down here to say hello the other night? I meant to say we came down here for a little nightcap. I just didn't want to get Frank and Bernard into hot water, you know? Thought we'd uh, get rid of the evidence, so to speak."

The boys nodded and grinned, sharing a conspiratorial look of their own.

"That Hamilton, he's a good kid," one of them said. "Never too good to come down here and, uh, 'say hello.'"

"Yeah, he can be cool like that."

The guards let me go, and I went outside and opened the Volvo's trunk. I rearranged the box of used books and the tire jack and the toolbox, and hid the tin can under my emergency blankets. There wasn't a bottle in there, of course; it was the videotape of Hamilton's father telling us he'd been poisoned. I couldn't leave it in the car for good—just the heat of a Tennessee summer afternoon could melt the thing—but I certainly wasn't going to bring it into the house until I had somewhere to hide it.

The 4x4 Claude had driven down to the police station was already parked out in front of the house when I drove up, which meant he'd hightailed it back here trying to beat me home. I left the car for the valet service and took the front steps three at a time. Crashing into the house and bolting

"There were clothes on the floor? Thrown around?"

"*Sí,*" he said with a nod.

Leave it to a Prince to tear somebody's room apart and then call in a servant to clean up afterwards. Claude had beaten me home not only to snag the last bottle of Johnnie Walker Hamilton's father had been drinking before he died—which I suspected was laced with the same weak poison he'd been drinking steadily for weeks, maybe months—but also to ransack my room looking for the videotape.

Game on, indeed.

Hamilton appeared at my door, his sunglasses barely hiding the huge black ring around his left eye.

"Hey," he said, still drowsy. "I've been looking everywhere for you." He saw the guy behind me folding clothes and putting them away. "What's he doing?"

"Cleaning up a mess I didn't make."

"Huh?"

"Nothing. What's up?"

"Claude and Trudy want to see me in his office."

"So go."

He stood and stared at me expectantly. I took a five-dollar bill out of my wallet and handed it to the help. He tried to turn it down, but I stuffed it in his shirt pocket and left with Hamilton.

"You don't have to tip them," Hamilton said in the hall. "They do get *paid,* you know."

"Not by me," I told him.

The dead bear on the floor of Claude's study sneered at us as we entered, and I bent down to scratch his head. Claude and Mrs. Prince were sitting in chairs in front of his desk, looking concerned. Hamilton dropped into a chair in the corner and exuded teen angst.

"Hamilton, this is a family meeting. Your friend can wait outside," Claude said, not looking at me.

Hamilton practiced not caring.

"Horatio, would you mind giving us some time alone with Hamilton?" Mrs. Prince asked.

I didn't mind telling Claude to sit and spin, but Mrs. Prince was another matter. I glanced at Hamilton.

"I want him here," said Hamilton. "I need at least one person in the room I can trust."

"That's a terrible thing to say to your mother," Claude told him.

"But not to you?"

"Hamilton, please take those sunglasses off when we're speaking to you," Mrs. Prince said. There must have been some small spark of love still there for his mother, because he did what she asked him.

Claude was startled by Hamilton's face. "Who gave you the shiner?"

"Was there something you wanted to say, or what?" said Hamilton.

Claude shifted in his chair and got frowny serious. "I just spent the afternoon taking care of your little stunt this morning, Hamilton. Luckily," he said, glancing my way for the first time, "I have friends in the department."

"Yeah," Hamilton said. "Lucky for a lot of reasons."

Mrs. Prince took a deep breath.

"Hamilton, I have no idea what happened to you this morning, or why you did what you did," she said. She glanced at Claude, probably remembering the part where Hamilton called her new husband a murderer. "But your behavior has gotten worse and worse. Paul Mendelsohn is in the *hospital,* and you came very near to—to—"

"You're out of control," said Claude. "And it has to stop."

Hamilton shot up straight in his chair. "*I'm* out of control?"

"Yes," Mrs. Prince told him. "And it doesn't help that you sit around and drink all day long."

So this was it, I thought. The intervention Claude was talking about. My little brain had been imagining all kinds of sinister meanings for what he said to Paul that night listening in over the intercom, and here they were giving him a real intervention.

"I saw this happen to your father too," said Claude.

Hamilton was on his feet. "Don't you dare! Don't you *dare* talk about my father!"

"Hamilton, sit down," Mrs. Prince said, surprising us all with the strength in her voice. *"Sit down."*

Hamilton dropped into his chair, but the sunglasses came back on.

"Your stepfather and I have decided that we are not capable of treating your illness."

"My illness?"

"There is a clinic near Bristol, just over the border into Virginia—"

"What kind of clinic?"

"An alcohol rehabilitation clinic," Claude told him. "You're an alcoholic, Hamilton, and you need to get better."

"I'm not an alcoholic!" He laughed. "Tell them, Horatio."

I crossed my arms and kept my mouth shut, and he didn't like that very much.

"You see, even your friends know you drink too much, Hamilton."

"If you'd just look at the brochure—" Mrs. Prince began.

Hamilton was up out of his chair. "No way I'm going to any 'clinic.'"

"I'm sorry," Claude said smoothly. "I don't remember anyone *asking* you."

Every one of us had seen the play before, but Hamilton put on an encore performance of *Kick a Chair and Storm Out of the Room*. If he wasn't careful he was going to get typecast.

"Horatio," Mrs. Prince pleaded. "You know this is right. Can you speak to him?"

She handed me the brochure and I glanced at it. It was full of inspirational gobbledygook like "The longest journey begins with the first step," and "Denial isn't just a river in Egypt," and had pictures of half-smiling teenagers silently wondering how they could hang themselves on the ropes course they were doing. I stuffed the pamphlet in my back pocket and looked at Claude, who was watching me. My accusation sat there between us, but he wasn't going to say anything with Mrs. Prince in the room. What concerned me was what he might say—or do—if he got me or Hamilton alone.

"We'll see," I said about the brochure. "I thought I might run into town and rent a video first." I gave Claude a sunshiny smile. "Anything you're dying to see, Claude?"

Mrs. Prince didn't know what I was talking about, but dark clouds formed on Claude's forehead and I beat a hasty retreat.

Hamilton wasn't out by the pool, and he wasn't in the entertainment room with Roscoe and Gilbert. I found him in his room, digging through his closet.

"Looking for something to drink?"

"Get out."

I sat down at his computer desk and watched.

"I said get out."

I put my feet up.

"Thanks a hell of a lot for sticking up for me back there."

"Hamilton, look. I'm your best friend—" I started.

He came out of the closet with a water bottle in his hand. He gave me a look that was supposed to make me feel bad for thinking the worst of him, but I snatched the bottle away before he could stop me.

"Hey!"

I unscrewed the cap and dipped a finger in to taste it. Vodka.

"Couldn't just pour out good vodka for your stunt with Roscoe and Gilbert, could you?"

"Wait, wait," he said. "Is this the part where you tell me I have a problem, and that you just want to see me get better? Screw you. I can take care of myself."

"Digging this out to throw it away, then?"

He grabbed the bottle back from me and told me to go do something to myself that was physically impossible. I said I'd pass.

"You think you're so smart, don't you, Horatio?"

"Smart enough to know you need help—in more ways than one."

"What's that supposed to mean?"

"Hamilton, Claude knows. He knows that we know he murdered your father. If he didn't get it when you plugged Paul Mendelsohn, he figured it out when he caught me down at the police station telling them about the videotape."

"You did *what?* Damn it, Horatio! Those bastards are in his pocket. They wouldn't help us."

"Yes, well, I realize that *now,*" I muttered.

"Besides, you promised! You swore you wouldn't tell a soul."

"Oh, give the secret society thing a rest, Hamilton. It's not kid stuff anymore when you shoot somebody."

"He's not dead," Hamilton said softly. He unscrewed the bottle cap and took a swig. He winced as he worked it down, then took another drink just to prove to his throat who was boss.

"No, he's not dead," I told him. "And he's not going to press charges either. But you and I both know you shot him because he was wearing your uncle's hunting vest and you thought it was Claude. And your uncle knows that too."

"So what?" he said. "Let him."

"Ordinarily I'd agree. But let's review, shall we? We agree that Claude murdered your father so he could take over Elsinore Paper. If he would kill for something like that, don't you think he'd kill again not to go to jail?"

Hamilton blinked. "You mean—you mean you think he might try to kill me?"

"Gee," I told him, "after you tried to do the same thing to him? I wonder."

"Wait," he said, panicking a little. "What am I going to do?"

"It seems to me they've handed you a way out."

I pulled the clinic brochure from my pocket and tossed it at him. It fluttered to the ground between us.

"No way, Horatio. I can't—"

"You can, and you should. First off, you'll be about a hundred miles away from Claude, in a safe and secure facility."

"A prison, you mean."

"You said your house and the plant were a prison, remember? What's the difference?"

He answered me by taking another drink.

"Second, you need it." I stood and took the bottle from him. "And yes, you do have a problem, and yes, I do want to see you get better."

"It's just this stuff with my dad—"

"That made it worse, yeah. But you don't drink for fun, Hamilton, and you don't drink to relax. You drink to drink."

He stared at the brochure on the floor at my feet.

"What about Claude? How can we bust him for murdering my father when I'm off in some sanatorium?"

"I'm not sure we can now," I told him. "But you won't leave for a few days. Give me one last chance to pull something off. It'll be tricky, but there might be something I can do. In the meantime, you pack your bags and watch your back. Deal?"

Hamilton sat quietly for longer than I was willing to count. "Deal."

CHAPTER NINETEEN

I left Hamilton in his room and got my car without waiting for a valet. For what I was cooking up, I needed to talk to Olivia. I couldn't have found her favorite mountaintop view again if I had a week to drive every back road in Denmark, and I didn't know where she lived. That left only one place I knew to try her, and I drove into town.

The banged-up door of the diner labeled only as "EATS" screeched across the linoleum as I stepped inside. It was the place where Olivia and I had gone on our first date, and the smell of grease and disinfectant made me all nostalgic. EATS was empty of customers, being post-lunch and pre-dinner rush, although I wondered if it didn't always look like this. I slid into the booth I liked to think of as "our booth" and set the coffee can I'd brought in on the seat beside me.

The dinosaur who had served us our meal the last time was standing behind the counter. A long, limp mound of ash dangled from the cigarette in her mouth as she skimmed over what was, no doubt, the newspaper want ads. She glanced up at me and registered my existence through lidded eyes.

"Liv," she called. "Table two." The ashes took a plunge from her cigarette, and she wiped them off her paper onto the counter.

The kitchen doors swung open, and Olivia walked out wearing an ugly blue waitress smock that still managed to look good on her somehow. What can I say? I'm a private-school kid. I love a girl in uniform.

She gave me a tired look like she could read my mind.

"Want me to take him, honey?" the crone asked.

"No thanks," Olivia decided. She walked my way and stood over me with her hands on her hips. "You miss me already?"

"Yeah," I told her. "You don't know it, but I saved one of my stained napkins from the time we came here together. I'm making a scrapbook for you."

"Shut up," she said. There was almost a grin there, but she had other things on her mind. "You want food or what?"

"Hamburger and fries was good. And a root beer."

She nodded and went back behind the counter to announce my order to the cook. She brought a root beer and a soda to the table and sat down across from me.

"Look, if you've come here to apologize for Hamilton—"

"He can do his own apologizing, for whatever it's worth," I said. "I hear your dad's going to be all right."

She nodded. "His shoulder's pretty messed up, and he'll be in the hospital for a while, but Hamilton didn't hit anything worse. Dad was lucky. . . ."

I had to agree. It was a strange kind of luck, but he had it.

"He's been asleep almost all day. They sent me home, but I couldn't go back to an empty house." She shrugged. "I was scheduled to work anyway, so I thought I'd come here. Larry will be home from school late tonight, and he can check in on Dad." She stirred the ice in her drink with her straw. "So how did you know I worked here?"

"Well, for one thing, the last time we were here you said you'd take care of the check, and we left without you paying. Cindy over there seemed to know you pretty well too, so unless you were planning on never showing your face here again, I figured you must work here."

"How did you know her name?"

I reached across the table and flicked the name badge pinned to Olivia's uniform.

"Well, aren't you the detective," she told me, but I could tell she was impressed.

A bell rang, and somebody in the back shouted, "Order up!" Olivia slid out of the booth and Cindy handed her my plate across the counter. She slid back into the booth and put the food between us and started eating my fries.

"So, why track me down?" she asked. "I'm sure the Prince family already knows my dad isn't going to have Hamilton arrested."

"You keep forgetting my last name isn't Prince. What I want and what they want are not always the same."

"And what is it you want, Horatio Wilkes?"

There were a hundred good answers to that one that might actually have gotten me somewhere, but it was time to get serious.

"You really want to see Elsinore pay for dumping in the Copenhagen River, don't you."

That was a direction she hadn't expected me to go, and she frowned. "Well, yeah. Of course. Why?"

"Because I agree. I think it's about time somebody made Elsinore accountable. Some of the Princes too."

"Some?"

"The ones who actively covered up the pollution."

She seemed to agree with that. "What, have you got something on them?"

"Maybe. But we're going to need a little help. What we've got to do is forget the *Daily Dane* and get some regional coverage, maybe even national."

"I've tried," Olivia told me between french fries.

"The Brown-Water Rafting thing was clever, but we've got to have something shocking. Something scandalous. You know how these TV news things go—'Something in your tap water may be killing you! Tune in at eleven.'"

She sipped on her Coke. "The trouble is, there's no way to prove that people get sick and die around here because of the pollution. They all die long, weary deaths. TV crews want to see a big car accident or a house burning down. Something happening right that minute. Nobody wants to come up here and film water running over rocks."

"What if we tell them somebody drank water from the river and got really sick?"

"You're kidding, right? Only a complete dumb-ass would drink that water."

"Right." I took her soda from her. "But you'd drink *this* on camera, wouldn't you?"

It didn't take much effort to shake a fizzy foam up to the surface of her Coke. Without the ice it looked just like the Copenhagen River.

"We put you in front of a camera, and you tell them you're going to drink river water to show how disgusting it is. You take a swig from a jar, make a big scene of spewing it back out, and we get a chance to talk about what they're doing to the water up here."

"And you think they're going to buy that?"

"Well, it *looks* like river water." I gave her the drink back.

"Maybe we could break up little bits of cake in it or something to give it some texture."

"Now I can't wait to do it," she said.

"Anyway, if they call us on it, they'll have already come all this way. They're not going to go back without a story, even a slow one like that nasty brown water churning away."

Olivia mulled that over while I finished my hamburger.

"Okay. And you want me to be the drinker?"

"I think I can get a station here, but you're the local interest. It's your cause. Your story. Besides, you're moderately better-looking than I am."

"Thanks for noticing. So what's in this for you?"

"I'm a sucker for a hopeless cause," I told her. "*And* I want to get my hands on Elsinore's pollution testing results. Claude's not in much of a mood to let me have a look at them, but if we can get some public pressure on the plant, maybe they'll have to release them."

"You think there's proof they've been poisoning the river in the test results?"

"No. I'll bet you're right—those tests are crooked, done wrong to make the plant look like it's in the clear with the EPA. I need them to prove that something else was poisoned instead."

"Like what?"

"Like Hamilton's father."

She was the second person I'd spilled the beans to that day, and I was beginning to think I should just post flyers that said "Somebody Murdered Rex Prince" instead of working my way through Denmark person by person. It was dangerous to bring her into this, for her sake and ours, but I figured Hamilton owed her that much, and a lot more.

"Hamilton's father?" she whispered. "You mean—"

I picked up the coffee can I had brought inside and slid it across the table to her.

"One more favor," I said. "Can you hide this somewhere for me? Someplace you can get to it again quickly? I can't keep it in my car or up at the house."

"Yeah, sure. I guess." She shifted it around, feeling now *two* clunky things shift around inside. "What's in it?"

"Evidence," I told her. "Just make sure it stays dry and room temperature, will you? I promise I'll explain everything when I can. And don't get curious and open it. Seriously. You do *not* want your fingerprints on either item."

"Secret agent man," she said.

We exchanged phone numbers, and I pulled out my wallet and left money for the meal.

"Forget the tip," she said. "I'm not poor or anything."

"No, but you work for your money, and you earned it. I'll call you when I get somebody to come out and film." I stood to leave. "And Olivia—" I said, meaning to follow it up with something else. An apology maybe, or an explanation, or something that would bring back that spark we'd once had.

"Thanks," I said instead, and I left before I could make anything worse.

CHAPTER TWENTY

—💀—

I took a particular delight in calling for Candy to bring me a root beer in my room, and once I explained what I was up to with Olivia he even cracked a smile. He was also kind enough to put in a discreet call to Ford Branff for me on Monday. Branff was a little suspicious at first, but he was a smart guy and got where I was going pretty quickly. He promised me we'd have a television crew over from one of his stations in Knoxville by the end of the week. Ford wasn't about to pass up a chance to rake some muck over Elsinore Paper International, and besides, cute girls puking their guts out apparently makes good TV, as evidenced by *Girls Gone Wild: Miami Beach* and its seventeen sequels.

Olivia sounded less than enthusiastic when I called her later that day, but said she'd be there. If she got cold feet we'd lose our money shot, but I figured I could do it if she chickened out.

In the meantime, plans for Hamilton's stay at the rehab clinic in Bristol moved quickly. Claude and Mrs. Prince pulled him in for another family meeting on Tuesday—this time without me—and told him D-day was Friday morning.

That left just three days before we were both gone, because it was clear from my hosts that I would be shipping out at the same time. Apparently Claude's answer to our snooping around was to get us both out of town as quickly as possible. They didn't get any complaints from me, but I worried there was too little time to get the dirt on Hamilton's uncle. Maybe the best I would be able to do would be to set the wheels in motion, but the thought didn't do anything to make my last days here smell any rosier.

The morning of Olivia's televised spit-take we met down by the river where the runoff pipe pumps the sludge into the Copenhagen River. She was already there when I arrived. She looked bad, like she really was sick, and I told her so.

"All part of the show," she told me, and she looked like she might throw up already just from the effort. If she was really sick it would look better for the cameras, but I worried there was more to it. Before I could press her on it, we saw the news crew looking for us on the road above the river and I ran to flag them down. They had sent a little compact hatchback with the channel number and call-letters plastered all over the outside of it. I helped the cameraman haul out a couple of boxes while the reporter spruced herself in the mirror.

"God, it stinks bad enough," the reporter said. "So the water is actually brown? If it's not dark enough, this stunt's probably not going to make the news, no matter who you know."

"Don't worry," I told her. "It's a real story."

"Jack, you think you'll have enough light?" she asked.

The cameraman consulted a light gauge and nodded. "I'll check it again by the river, but yeah." I led them through the brush and trees down to the water, where Olivia sat on a rock. She stood to say hello, and I could see her sway a little. Had she been drinking? Was that why she looked so sick?

"You think we should make her up a little first?" the woman whispered.

Her cameraman shook his head. "Nah. This'll sell it better anyway."

Then they got a good look at that river, and it was like they had discovered the lost Fountain of Youth and it was a sewer.

"God, look at it, Jack! It's disgusting! Do you think you can get a shot of that part there, where it's all bubbling up? Is that where it comes from the factory?"

"Plant," Olivia corrected her. She swallowed like she was holding down a couple of meals and managed to give the reporter a brief history of the situation.

"Great—wait," the woman said. "Let Jack get the camera set up before you tell me everything, and we'll go through it before you drink the water."

I pulled Olivia aside while we waited.

"What's up with you? Are you all right?" I asked.

She nodded sluggishly.

"Have you been drinking?" I whispered.

"Kind of," she said.

"Okay, we're ready," the reporter said. "If you can just stand here." She guided Olivia to a picturesque spot with the chunky brown water behind them. Olivia might have looked drunk, but she was sharp as ever. I knew a good sound bite when I heard one, and she gave them half a dozen. The reporter was clearly impressed too. She kept sharing knowing looks with the cameraman, who returned them with a thumbs-up.

"Now, I understand you're going to drink some river water today," the reporter prompted her, "as a protest against what you perceive to be illegal pollution levels here in the Copenhagen River."

Olivia nodded. "That's right. Elsinore Paper claims this water is safe, and the EPA agrees with them. I'm here to show everybody they're both wrong."

Olivia pulled a Mason jar out of the pocket of her Windbreaker and held it up in front of the camera. From where I stood, it didn't look like soda. It looked like tea mixed with cleaning detergent and whipped into a frothy soup. In fact, it looked like river water.

"Now, how can we be sure that's really water from the river?" the reporter asked. "I mean, who's to say you didn't just go to a convenience store and mix together all the sodas?"

Olivia glanced at me, and it felt like an apology. I couldn't figure out the look, since we'd planned for this all along anyway. I started to step forward to explain everything, but she looked back into the eye of the camera and said, "It's river water, all right, and I've been drinking it nonstop for three days."

I stopped in my tracks. She couldn't be serious.

"Here, I'll prove it," she said. She unscrewed the jar and poured it out, then dipped the jar into the river and pulled up an equally foamy broth.

My feet were moving before my mouth. "No, Olivia! Don't—"

I was too far away. She took a big hit off the stuff, and it immediately came back up, along with half a gallon of whatever else she had to eat and drink in the last few hours. I caught her in my arms as she collapsed to the ground, letting her cough the rest of it out. I couldn't believe I'd been so stupid.

"You did it for real, didn't you," I said.

"No point in—sending them home without a story."

Olivia lurched and her stomach erupted again. I held her

up and pulled my phone out to dial 911, beginning to feel like I was doing this a little too often lately.

Out of range. Again.

The reporter had backed off from the puke zone, but the cameraman hadn't left his place. "Hey kid," he asked, "is she faking it?"

"No, she's not faking it!" I yelled. "Now turn that thing off and help me get her to the hospital!"

CHAPTER TWENTY-ONE

—💀—

I hate hospitals. The hushed whispers of sympathy, the sad, flickering televisions in dark rooms, the lingering scent of antiseptic and vomit. Zombies ambling around in those gowns where everyone can see their asses, clinging to wheeled coatracks with plasma or saline or something dripping into their veins. Sneakers *squeak squeak squeaking* down the hall as nurses deliver little cups of meds and trays with lumps that resemble mashed potatoes and Salisbury steak. But worse than all that was the feeling of weakness. Vulnerability.

Helplessness.

I had been here almost the entire day, waiting while doctors whisked Olivia away to an operating room where her stomach was pumped and she was rehydrated with water that wasn't brown. When they were finished, they put her in a hospital room right next to her father. That made things pretty convenient for Larry Mendelsohn, I thought, although he didn't seem to see it that way. I also thought that as a future ambulance-chaser he'd appreciate the opportunity to scare up some prospective clients, but for some reason Larry didn't act like any of this was convenient. He acted like he was mad at the world, starting with me.

"Five minutes," he told me when I tried to get in to see Olivia.

As the guy who dragged his sister to the hospital I thought I might get to spend a little more time with her, but Larry the lawyer had laid down the law. He went next door to give us some privacy, which I guess was as much of a nod to me saving her life as I was going to get.

Olivia looked like she'd gone three rounds with a gorilla. A tube as thick as my middle finger snaked down her nose, and she had the makings of two black eyes worse than the one she'd given Hamilton. She played it tough and mustered a grin when she saw me.

"Hey."

"Hey yourself," I told her. "You know, if you wanted to lose weight, I can think of a few easier ways."

"Who says I need to lose weight?"

She was weaker than she was letting on, and I figured the five minutes Larry gave me would probably be about two minutes longer than she could keep this up. I sat down in the chair next to the bed.

"Now, let's see . . . " I said. "Who was it that said that only a complete dumb-ass would drink that water?"

"You're welcome," she wheezed. "Finally did it, though, didn't I?"

Olivia nodded at the television hanging from the ceiling. She had just found a regional news feed from Knoxville, and they were leading off with the story of the high school environmental activist who got violently sick drinking "clean" river water. Local community leaders were shocked—*shocked!*—to discover their river was so polluted, and there were rumblings about an emergency session of the Denmark city council.

Olivia closed her eyes. "Mission accomplished."

"You really scared me, you know that? I dreamed about taking you in my arms one day, but not to the hospital."

"Be careful, Horatio. Hamilton might be around to hear you."

"You could have *died*," I told her.

"Died?" said a doctor coming in the room. He consulted a boxy metal clipboard. "No, she wasn't in danger of dying. Making herself very, very, sick, yes, but not dying. The pollution in the river is too diluted for that. You'd have to extract a large quantity of dioxin and drink a concentrated dose to do immediate harm."

He wasn't the fellow I had handed Olivia off to in the emergency room, but the way he was checking her medical folder against the beeping machines along the wall meant he'd gotten involved somewhere along the way. I was more interested in that medical folder. It was giving me ideas.

"Are you feeling any numbness?" he asked Olivia. "Any strange sensations in your extremities? Does anything hurt?"

"I'm not sure, but I think there's something wrong with my nose," she said, pointing to the huge tube jammed down her throat. The doctor smiled sympathetically.

"That has to stay there until you're released."

"When will that be? Tonight?"

"No—I'm sorry. We're going to want to keep you overnight for observation."

"What was it in the water that made her so sick?" I asked.

"A variety of things caused these symptoms, but the compound we're most concerned about, of course, is dioxin.

That's the main reason for the stomach pump and the infusion of olestra." He turned to Olivia. "The olestra bonds with the dioxin, which should help you pass most of it out."

Olivia got a mental picture of passing olestra and grimaced.

"Dioxin is a poison?" I asked. I was developing an interest in poisons too.

The doctor folded his arms across Olivia's medical chart. "Dioxin may be the most toxic substance ever created by man."

I didn't think it was possible, but Olivia got whiter.

"What could it do?" she rasped.

"Dioxin is a carcinogen. It causes cancer. The more that's left in your system, the greater your chance of getting cancer one day."

"Can you get it all out?" I asked.

"Well, even if we were able to remove all the dioxin she ingested over the last few days, she'd still have dioxin in her system. Just about every person in America tested for the stuff has five to ten parts per trillion of dioxin in their bodies, and we haven't got the slightest idea where it comes from."

"That's always a good thing to hear from a doctor."

He shrugged. "Dioxin is almost a complete unknown. There have been all kinds of tests on lab animals, of course, but each study comes out differently. One animal gets liver cancer. Another gets lung cancer. Another gets stomach cancer. But one thing remains the same in each case."

"They all get cancer," I guessed.

He nodded. "That's why dioxin is thought to be the most toxic chemical in creation—it can cause cancer in just trace amounts."

"Does that mean—does that mean I'm going to get cancer?" Olivia asked.

"Twenty to twenty-five percent of Americans develop some kind of cancer," he told her. "Each of us carries more than trace amounts of dioxin, and we're exposed to countless other carcinogens every day. They're in the air we breathe, the food we eat, even the cups and napkins we use. Once we clean you up, I'd say your chances are about the same as anyone else's."

The doctor checked a few more things on Olivia's chart, then flipped it closed.

"I hope I haven't scared you," he said.

"No more than I already was," Olivia croaked.

He smiled. "You're going to be fine. This is the worst of it right now. Just promise me no more stunts like the one you pulled this morning."

"Okay, twist my arm," she joked.

Larry caught the doctor at the door and got the whole spiel again. It bought me a few minutes more with Olivia, and I got up to stand by her side. I moved a strand of hair off her face and held her hand.

"You really are a dumb-ass," I told her.

"Thanks," she said. "I kind of like you too."

"Look, about that day, on the bluff," I told her. "I wanted to. Really. It wasn't you—"

"I know. It wasn't me, it was Hamilton." She laughed, and it turned into a cough.

Larry heard her coughing and came in looking as unhappy about me holding her hand as Olivia poisoning herself. He folded his arms across his chest.

"Time's up," he told me.

"I'll be back tomorrow," I promised Olivia. "And don't

worry," I told Larry on the way out, "no rich little hotties have ever fawned over me at Wittenberg."

Larry shut the door behind me.

I peeked in at Paul Mendelsohn. He was sleeping soundly. On the screen above him, Olivia was watching over him through the miracle of cable and sound bites as the story of her poisoning ran on a twenty-four-hour cable news station. Her pale face on the TV reminded me of Hamilton's father, coming to us live as a ghost from the valley of death.

Thinking of Hamilton's father made medical charts come to mind again, and it didn't take me long to find a nurse's station. The only woman there was youngish—midtwenties, maybe—with mousy brown hair and a bit of an overbite.

"Help you?" she asked.

"Hi," I said, putting on my sad face. "My name is Hamilton Prince. My dad was a patient here a while back, but I can't remember the name of his doctor."

"He can't tell you?" she asked.

"He died of cancer," I told her. "While I was away at school. I'm supposed to talk to his doctor. To, you know, get some kind of closure."

"I'm so sorry," she said. "You don't have any bills or medical records at home? Doesn't your mother have his name?"

"My mother died last year. Car wreck." I sniffed and blinked my eyes, getting them wet. "I'm sorry. The school psychiatrist gave me the name before the summer break, but everything's been so crazy . . ."

I was laying it on pretty thick, but I could see her weak chin get weaker.

"Prince, you said? What was his first name?" she asked, swiveling to her computer.

"Hamilton. Just like—just like me."

She nodded, then scribbled the name on a pad advertising a blue pill with a funny name and passed it across the counter to me.

"Dr. Henry Lapham," she told me. "He won't be back in until next week."

"Thanks," I said. I sniffed again for effect. "I guess I was so messed up then, I just wasn't thinking."

"See it all the time," she told me. "You call his office and have your chat."

I thanked her again and kept up the sniffling until I was around the corner, then headed down the hall to a room I had passed on the way in. A little green plaque on the wall read: "Records Room." I glanced around to see that no one was around, and I slipped inside.

The last time there was a presidential election, there was a lot of hullabaloo about fixing health care. Part of that, apparently, was the idea that all the hospitals in the country would keep patient records on computers so they could be shared anytime, anywhere. Luckily for me, nothing ever got done about it. Everybody still keeps files the old-fashioned way—in easy-to-steal paper folders.

I scanned the wall of floor-to-ceiling shelves and quickly found the P's. I had always seen these rainbow-colored folders behind the reception desk at my dentist, but only when I was close up did I realize that the colors corresponded to different letters of the alphabet, I guess so the medical professionals could thumb through them quickly. It worked too—I found Rex Prince's file in no time. It was pretty thick, and there were reports from a number of doctors over the years inside. I caught Dr. Henry Lapham's signature at the bottom of one or two pages and knew I had what I was looking for. I debated just taking the ones I needed, but figuring that out would take time. Besides, Mr. Prince wasn't going to be visiting his doctor anytime soon, so I just took the whole thing.

The trick to stealing something is to just walk out with it like you're supposed to be taking it. My sister Miranda, who's a patrol cop in Knoxville, once told me about two thieves who went into a sporting goods store, picked up a canoe, and carried it right out the front door. Security cameras caught it and tons of people saw them, but they got away with it because nobody thought they were stealing it. One of the clerks actually held the *door* open for them. After all, who just walks out with a canoe without paying for it?

The color-coding on the edge of the folder was the only thing that might have given me away, so I kept that part tucked under my arm. I nodded to a nurse or two as I left, humming a They Might Be Giants tune and acting nonchalant. It was smooth sailing the rest of the way out to my car, and I thought—not for the first time—that were I not a young man of extraordinary personal character, I could have made a lot of money in this world as a con man.

At least it was something to fall back on.

CHAPTER TWENTY-TWO

I went through a drive-thru to get myself my first real food of the day. The burger paled in comparison to the two I'd had where Olivia worked, but it was edible. Scanning for Dr. Lapham's name, I pored over the medical file in my lap. The scrawl on them was nearly illegible, but I wouldn't have been able to understand what I was looking at even if they had been printed off a computer. It was all doctor gobbledygook, but a word I translated as *dioxin* did manage to show up here and there.

Olivia's doctor had told her that river water was still too diluted to really kill anybody—at least quickly. I remembered him saying there was dioxin in almost everything, and I suddenly lost my appetite for the rest of my french fries. What if Mr. Prince really *had* died of cancer—cancer brought on by high levels of dioxin? Technically that qualified as poison, though not the fastest or surest poison in the world. But who said Claude Prince was in a hurry? Still, I needed to know exactly what these records said, or it was all just guesswork.

A convenience store across the street advertised, among the many ads for beer, cigarettes, and lottery tickets, that they had a fax machine. I slid the Volvo into crawl and drove over.

A guy with about three good teeth grinned at me as I came in.

"You got a fax?" I asked him.

"Four dollars a page, coming or going."

"Four dollars a page? That's highway robbery."

The fellow grinned again. "'S the only one in town, kid."

I couldn't argue with Toothy's grasp of supply and demand theory, so I put the pages on the counter and ponied up the sixteen bucks this was going to cost me. Perhaps I would walk out the front door of the Prince mansion with Hamilton's PlayStation in hand as a return on my investment. I waited while the clerk fed the pages into the world's oldest existing fax machine. The paper tray was almost empty, and while he was at it he cracked open a brand-new ream of Elsinore International paper to fill it.

I looked around, thinking about how ubiquitous paper was. Every cereal box, every waxed-paper package, every napkin and tissue and magazine—it didn't all come from Elsinore, but enough did. And inside each and every one there was dioxin, the unusable, highly toxic by-product of making paper. In trace amounts, to be sure. The kind of trace amounts that made mouse spleens grow ten times their size and explode. It was probably in everything in this town, from the river to the paper to the food.

"You need anything else?" the clerk asked.

"Yeah," I said, turning around. "Where's your bottled water?"

Back at the ranch, I returned to my room and dialed my sister Rosalind.

Rosalind skipped the hellos when she heard my voice. "Horatio! Where have you been? We've all been trying to get in touch with you."

"Is anything wrong?" I asked.

"No, of course not, but—"

"Then the One Hundred Constructive Ways for Horatio to Spend His Summer Vacation can wait a few more days at least. They're kicking me out early."

"What did you do?"

The way she said that made it sound like it had only been a matter of time. I was hurt.

"The usual stuff," I told her. "Told the truth, fought for justice, made the ladies fall in love."

"You met some girls?"

"Just one, but she took my hat and puked on my Converse. Did you get that fax I just sent?"

"Clark's looking it over now." The phone muffled like it had slid off her shoulder. "No, that says two thousand parts per trillion," I heard her tell him.

Rosalind and her husband, Clark, were both doctors, and they were always on me to eat healthy. We'll get into what kind of name "Clark" is another time.

"Horatio, I don't know who your friend is here, but he's got enough dioxin in him to kill him."

"Too late," I told her. "But the dioxin itself wouldn't kill him, would it?"

"No," she said, and I could hear the questions mounting. "Dioxin causes cancer. It probably led to this." I heard the shuffling of papers. "Your friend had liver cancer *and* intestinal cancer."

There was murmuring in the background, and Rosalind came back on the line. "Clark says he probably would have had chloracne too. It'll make you look like you're a hundred years old and made of granite."

Bingo.

"Horatio, where did you get these files? What have you gotten yourself into?"

"Science fair project," I told her. "Thanks, Roz. Say hey to Superman for me."

I hung up before she could say anything more, and considered that being out of area was still good for something. Unless Roz had caller ID, I realized suddenly. If she did, the household staff at Chez Prince was about to take a thousand messages.

So. Hamilton's father was poisoned by dioxin from his own pollution. The irony did not escape me, but I doubted it was intentional, since Claude was behind all this. That meant that it had to be a matter of convenience, not cleverness, that made the dioxin the poison of choice. What were the three things TV detectives always looked for? Motive, means, and opportunity. Motive: Become the older brother he always wanted to be and rule Elsinore. As a bonus, he'd even found a way to marry his brother's wife. Means: dioxin. But Rex Prince wasn't dense enough to drink river water, and the stuff was too diluted to begin with. So where did Claude get the concentrated stuff? His opportunity: every Friday night, slipping it into Rex Prince's favorite drink—Johnnie Walker Black Label whisky, neat.

Neat, indeed. If Hamilton's father died of cancer, there was almost no way to prove that it came from something Claude did to him. There were plenty of other things that could cause cancer of the liver and intestine, things we were all apparently eating and drinking and wiping ourselves with every day.

I crossed my arms and tapped my lips as I thought, then realized I was being watched from the doorway. It was Roscoe. Or Gilbert. I didn't really care which.

"Dude," he said, and he gave me a little clucking sound as he disappeared.

CHAPTER TWENTY-THREE

—💀—

Hamilton was already packed and ready to leave when I laid it all out for him. The medical report, the Friday night drinking, the effects of concentrated dioxin.

"You mean that's what did that to his face?"

"It's called chloracne," I told him. "It's evidence of dioxin poisoning."

Hamilton sat down on his bed and stared at the wall.

"I believed him. Dad, I mean. I just—I guess I kind of didn't believe him too."

"Believe it," I told him. "I've got all the evidence in a safe place."

"What do we do now?"

"You head off to Lake Onedrinktoomany Summer Camp and kick the habit. That was part of the deal. Meanwhile, I hop in the Volvo and drive straight to my sister Miranda's apartment."

"Which one is she?"

"The one who's a patrolwoman for the Knoxville Police Department. The cops here aren't worth their tin badges, but maybe we can get the state troopers or the Tennessee Bureau of Investigation involved. Worst-case scenario, you fax me your credit card number, and we hire a private detective to fill in the blanks."

Hamilton digested all that, then pulled out his wallet and handed me a gold AmEx. "Here. Go ahead and take it. It's in my name, not Claude's or Trudy's. They can't cut it off."

The little Roman soldier on the card stared back at me, and I could hear him whispering all the places we could go before someone did cut it off. If it weren't for that personal character thing. . . .

I pocketed the card and nodded.

"Man, I wish I could be here to see it," he said.

"I'll send you a postcard. In the meantime, you'll get clean and sober, and when you return, Elsinore will be all yours."

"I don't want Elsinore," he told me. "I want my dad back."

"I know, man. If there were any other reason, I wouldn't have done any of this."

Hamilton stood. He held out his hand, and I shook it.

"A deal's a deal," he told me. "I think I'll be safer strapped to my bed up there anyway."

"I don't think they do that anymore, strap people to beds," I said. We hauled our bags downstairs. "Electroshock to the nipples, maybe, but not leather straps on the beds."

"Thanks. You know where we're going?"

Claude and Mrs. Prince were due at a charity auction in Denmark that day, so I had volunteered to drive Hamilton to the clinic since I had to leave the house anyway. It was about two hundred miles out of my way, round-trip, but I figured it was the least I could do for convincing Hamilton to go. It also meant two more days away from my sisters.

I patted my pocket. "The brochure has directions."

It looked like the end of the party for Roscoe and Gilbert

too. They were throwing a few two-liters of glow-in-the-dark soda in the front seat when we came outside. Oddly, Claude and Mrs. Prince were there with them.

"You two guys leaving?" Hamilton asked.

"Leaving? We're driving you!" the thin one said with a laugh.

"Hamilton, I've asked these boys to take you to the facility for us," Claude said. "We trust them. They're old friends of the family."

My Spidey-sense went crazy. Something stank here, worse than the river.

"'Old friends of the family'? What the hell does that mean?" Hamilton demanded. "I had gym class with them in sixth grade!"

"It's really no trouble," I told his parents.

"You've already done so much," Mrs. Prince told me. She took my hand. Her skin felt like the warm rays of the sun.

"I want Horatio to take me," Hamilton persisted.

"It's already settled," Claude told him. There was a hard edge to his voice, and I wondered if we weren't being told to take the out he was giving us and be grateful for it.

"It's all right, I guess," I told Hamilton, though my eyes never left Claude's face. It was no surprise that Claude wanted his stepson to have nothing more to do with me, and I didn't want something like this to make Hamilton back out. "I'll come visit you after you get settled and bring you some cigarettes. They're like money on the inside."

"Thank you, Horatio," Mrs. Prince said. "You're a good friend."

"At least I have *one*," Hamilton groused. He tossed his bags into the trunk of the twins' Dodge Charger. "What do you guys get out of this?"

"Brand-new supercharger!" Gilbert said.

"Mr. Prince paid for it and installed it himself!" said Roscoe.

"That's right," I said to Claude. "You did mechanic work for Elsinore for a while, didn't you?" Then, as though I had just thought of it, "And weren't you a chemist too?"

I thought he'd glare, but instead he smiled, which was creepier.

"Good-bye, Horatio," he said, not deigning to shake hands. "Perhaps next time Hamilton can visit *you*."

"Yeah," I said. "Here's hoping."

Claude turned and smiled at Roscoe and Gilbert. "Now, I trust you boys'll remember to wait until you are safely on the open highway before you break a hundred with that supercharger."

"Wooo!" Roscoe yelled, and Gilbert gave him one of those weak knuckle-taps.

I went to give Hamilton one last handshake. "See you around, pal."

He took my hand and then pulled me into a shameless hug. I'm proud to say I'm secure enough in my sexuality that I hugged him back.

"Thanks for everything, Horatio. I'll never forget this."

Roscoe and Gilbert shook their heads. "Dude," one of them muttered.

"Get out of here," I told Hamilton. "I have to go wind up the rubber band in the Volvo."

He climbed in the backseat of their car, and with a rousing air-horn rendition of "Dixie" the Charger tore off down the driveway. As I watched them go, I mused that the only thing that would really keep them from hitting a hundred before the interstate was the windy, hilly road that corkscrewed through the mountains from here to there.

Mrs. Prince turned and walked back up the stairs to the house, leaving me alone with Claude. He stepped closer.

"I know you think otherwise, Horatio, but I didn't have anything to do with my brother's death," he told me. "Is that clear?"

"Clear as the Copenhagen River," I said.

I expected something nasty from him, but instead he just smiled like a fat man at an all-you-can-eat buffet. A cold, dark pit opened up in the bottom of my stomach, and I headed for my car. Claude decided it would be fun to stand and watch me leave, or else he just wanted to make sure I really *was* leaving. He even gave me a cheery wave when I glanced back at him in the rearview mirror. Was he really so smug that he thought he was going to get away with it?

But there had to be something more to it than that. Long after I had left the Prince estate, I could still see his grinning wave in the rearview mirror. Why had I let Roscoe and Gilbert be the ones to drive Hamilton to the clinic? I shook my head and focused on the twisting road. What did I think Roscoe and Gilbert were going to do, kill him? I was being ridiculous. Hamilton was out of Claude's clutches now, and that was all that was important.

Some of my friends have called me a slow driver. I prefer to say I am a deliberate driver. For all its age and lack of punch, the Volvo handles like a dream and I make a point of giving it my attention when I drive. I settled back and lost myself in the curves of the road. I had one stop to make before I hit the interstate—to visit Olivia in the hospital, find out where she'd hidden the coffee can I gave her, and say good-bye—and then I could trade this insanity for a different variety at home.

Still, I couldn't shake the feeling that sending Hamilton off with Roscoe and Gilbert was the wrong thing to do, if only because they weren't the sort you wanted as the last friendly faces you saw before you went into detox. There was no way to catch them now if I wanted to, but why couldn't I follow them and see Hamilton as soon as he was allowed visitors? As far as my family was concerned, I was still at Hamilton's house, and I could easily rent a room at a motel near the clinic for a couple of days. It was the least I could do.

I pulled the brochure out of my pocket and dialed the number on my cell phone. To my surprise, the call actually went through.

"St. Gregory's Drug and Alcohol Rehabilitation Clinic. This is Sandra. May I help you?"

"Yeah. Hi. My name's Horatio Wilkes, and my friend Hamilton Prince is checking in this afternoon. I don't know what the clinic's policy is on visits, but I was hoping to be able to drop in and say hello. You know, kind of as moral support. Will he be able to receive visitors anytime soon?"

I waited, but she didn't answer. Did she put me on hold?

"Hello? Hello?"

Nothing. I glanced at the screen on the phone. *Damn.* I had gone out of area in the middle of the call. I redialed the number, and this time it didn't even go through; I was still out of area. I flipped the phone closed and concentrated on my driving. A few minutes later I looked again. Two bars—worth a shot.

"St. Gregory's Drug and Alcohol Rehabilitation Clinic. This is Sandra. May I help you?"

"Hey. This is Horatio Wilkes again. Sorry, I'm calling from my cell, and I must have lost you. I don't know how much you got, but my friend Hamilton Prince is checking in this afternoon and—"

"Mr. Wilkes, I'm sorry to interrupt, but I double-checked

before you called back. We have no one staying here by that name."

I frowned, trying to understand this new information.

"Are you still there?" she asked.

"Uh, yeah. I'm here. Sorry. It's just weird, because I was told he's checking in today. Hamilton Prince. Like Princess without the –*ess*. You're sure?"

"I'm sorry, no Hamiltons, and no Princes. Trust me, I've been waiting all my life for a prince to come."

It was a good line, and on another day I might have laughed. Instead I thanked her, flipped my phone closed, and pulled off the road to think.

If Hamilton wasn't checking into the rehab clinic today, just where *were* Roscoe and Gilbert taking him?

Claude's wolflike grin and silly good-bye wave were all I could see, and suddenly it all made sense. I floored the Volvo and scrambled for my phone as I pulled out onto the road, sure I was right.

Roscoe Grant and Gilbert Stern were going to kill my best friend.

CHAPTER TWENTY-FOUR

I pushed the Volvo as fast as it could go, which wasn't saying much. There was no way I was going to catch up to them, and I didn't know exactly what I would do if I could. Still, I had to stop that car and get Hamilton out of it somehow, and calling the cops would be pointless.

With one hand I scrolled through my saved numbers and dialed Hamilton's cell phone.

Out of area.

A squirrel ran across the road in front of me, and I swerved to miss it. Even nature was against me.

"Come on, come on," I muttered, hitting redial. It was ringing! It was ringing—and then it wasn't. I cursed and considered hurling the damn thing out the window, but that wouldn't have helped much. I tried it again—out of area. Well, if Hamilton died, it was his own damn fault for living in the sticks.

I calmed down and tried to watch where I was driving. There was no sense in panicking. Either I would catch him or I wouldn't, and I had to be ready if I did. I took a deep breath and dialed his phone again.

It rang. He picked up.

"Horatio? Have you been trying to call? My phone kept ringing and—"

"Hamilton, shut up," I interrupted. "I need you to get out of the car."

"What? What are you talking about? We're almost to the interstate."

For a moment, I considered telling him everything, then I realized that was a bad idea. What if *he* panicked? There was nothing to stop Roscoe and Gilbert from pulling off down some side road and taking care of him. I had to get Hamilton out of that car without letting his "escorts" know I was onto them.

"You left something back at the house," I improvised. But what was the most indispensable thing he owned? "Your iPod."

"No I didn't. I packed it in my suitcase. I'm sure of it."

"One of the help found it on your desk when she went in to clean up. You must have forgotten."

"But I could swear—"

"*Hamilton,* I have it right here," I lied. "Can you find someplace to stop so I can get it back to you? You don't want to be stuck at that clinic for weeks without tunes."

"Yeah. Hang on." There was a muffled conversation, and then Hamilton was back on the line. "The guys are hungry anyway. There's a fast-food place right across from the motel at the interstate. You know the one?"

"Yeah, I spent the night in a ditch there once," I told him. "Listen, Hamilton, no matter what you do, don't let them take you anywhere else. And stay where people can see you."

"Horatio, man, don't be so intense. It's just an iPod."

I flipped my phone closed and spent the rest of the trip trying to figure out how exactly I was going to pry Hamilton away from two hired killers.

The Dodge Charger was in the parking lot of the fast-food joint, which was a relief. I hated lying to Hamilton on the phone, but it was for his own good. I hoped. I parked where I could make a quick getaway if I had to and fished around in the glove compartment for my electric razor. I kept it in the car for emergency shaves when I was late to school, even though in the year I had been driving I had neither been late to school nor ever had enough stubble to shave. Maybe now I would finally get some use out of the thing.

It was an older model, a hand-me-down from my father, with a round top that you ran along your skin so the cutters underneath could yank your hairs out. I stripped the protective metal cover off to reveal the cutting mechanism underneath and considered it. Not great, but it was all I had. I stuffed the razor in my pocket and headed inside.

It wasn't quite lunchtime, and Hamilton, Roscoe, and Gilbert were the only customers in the restaurant. They sat underneath a kind of glass sunroom slapped on the front of the dining area. The windows were still foggy around the edges from the morning dew. All three of them had trays with burgers, fries, and drinks, and Hamilton was just unwrapping his burger.

Pulling out the electric razor, I slid into the chair alongside the thin one—Roscoe?—and stuck it into his side.

"You ever been hit with a stun gun?" I asked him, just loud enough for the others at the table to hear me. "This one will pump a hundred thousand watts of juice into your muscles. In just a couple of seconds, your face will be in that burger and you'll need a clean change of underwear. You or your friend there so much as moves, and I pull the trigger."

Roscoe and Gilbert froze, and from the frightened looks on their faces, I thought they might have downloaded in their pants already.

"Horatio! What the hell—" Hamilton said, but I didn't want to get into it.

"Just get up from the table, Hamilton, and get into my car. I'll explain everything when we're gone."

"Have you gone nuts?" Hamilton asked.

"Just get in the car," I said, jamming my "Taser" into Roscoe's side just to remind him I was there. Hamilton stood and collected his food.

"Dude," said Gilbert. "Does this mean we don't get to keep the supercharger?"

I got up and shoved Hamilton out the door and toward my car. I glanced over my shoulder, but Roscoe and Gilbert were just sitting at the table talking animatedly.

I stuffed Hamilton into the passenger seat of my Volvo. "Hey, my stuff's in their trunk."

"You can use that gold AmEx you gave me to buy a new wardrobe. Get in."

The Volvo lurched out of the parking lot, and I hit the on-ramp for the highway.

"Where are we going? What's going on? *Horatio*—"

"The rehab clinic doesn't have any record of a Hamilton Prince checking in today. Or ever."

Hamilton stopped in mid-bite of his hamburger.

"Whah?"

"I called to see when I could visit you, and they had never heard of you. It's a trap. A fake-out. Roscoe and Gilbert weren't hired to take you to St. Gregory's. They were hired to kill you."

"Horatio, you can't be serious. Those two can't order fast food without looking at the pictures."

"You don't have to be smart to kill somebody. Just willing."

I took the razor out of my pocket and tossed it in the cup holder. Hamilton picked it up and looked at it.

"Don't you think you might be overreacting a bit?" he asked. "I mean, what if they booked me under a false name?"

"What, to keep it a secret from your fan club?"

"Because they're embarrassed for the family!"

I shook my head. "Your uncle was up to something. When I left he was smiling like he'd won the lottery."

"You leaving does have that effect on people, you know." Hamilton turned the razor over in his hands. "Wait a minute. Is this that razor you keep in the glove compartment? You rescued me with an electric razor!?" He clicked it on, but nothing happened. "It doesn't even work!"

"And that would have made it better somehow?" I asked. I took the razor from him and tossed it back in my glove box.

Hamilton shook his head. "You know, I thought *I* was bad, Horatio, but you're paranoid, man. You really thought Roscoe and Gilbert were going to kill me?" He put a foot on the dashboard and ate a french fry. "Not that I'm complaining about missing out on the drunk tank. So where are we going?"

"Knoxville. My house. We'll be safe there."

"Sure. If only because those two wacky killers can't read the road signs to get there."

"It's a shame," I told him. "You know, I think I finally had those two figured out."

"What, you mean why they were at the house?"

"No, which one is which."

"You're crazy," Hamilton said, and he went back to his lunch.

Something in the rearview mirror caught my eye, and I straightened.

"Maybe I'll get a chance to test out their names after all," I told him.

"Huh?"

I nodded back over my shoulder. The Dodge Charger was just coming over the rise in the road.

"They're probably just checking out that new supercharger," Hamilton said. "God. It was all they could talk about."

Roscoe and Gilbert were coming up fast. I glanced at the speedometer. I was doing a shaky seventy, and they were gaining on us like we were walking. Hamilton watched over his shoulder.

"They must be doing close to a hundred!"

The Charger got closer, closer, closer—it looked like they were going to ram us. My hands tightened on the steering wheel, but there was nowhere to go. The car was on top of us, and then it suddenly swung into the other lane and blew past, the boys whooping and hollering and blaring their "Dixie" horn.

Hamilton exhaled. "See? They're just joyriding. You're completely paranoid."

Ten car lengths ahead, the Dodge Charger burst into flames.

It swerved, then plunged into the grass median and exploded, showering the road with twisted metal and rubber.

I flattened the brake pedal and sent Hamilton's fries to the floor. Another explosion ripped through the trunk of their car, lifting it like a skirt in the wind. The Charger was a complete fireball.

There was no way either Roscoe or Gilbert could have survived.

"Dude," I said.

For a few seconds we watched the thick, nasty clouds of smoke billowing from the car, mesmerized by the impossibility of what we were seeing.

I handed Hamilton my cell phone.

"Here. Dial 911," I said, still unable to take my eyes off the charred wreckage.

"I can't," Hamilton said. He showed me the phone. "We're out of area."

CHAPTER TWENTY-FIVE

—💀—

The fiery demise of Roscoe and Gilbert meant Knoxville was now out of the question.

If Claude was willing to blow up a car with two innocent bystanders in it to get to his stepson, I wasn't about to put Hamilton up with my family. That would be the first place Claude would look for us anyway, and I didn't want to make things that easy.

Hamilton opened the motel room door and I dragged my bag inside. Neither of us had said much since the "accident," and he hadn't given me any more grief about being paranoid. I regretted not sticking around for the police report, but we could come forward with what we knew later. For now, it didn't hurt for the Prince family to think Hamilton had died in the flaming wreck. Forensics would tell them soon enough he wasn't in the car with Roscoe and Gilbert, but I figured it might buy us a day or two.

"I can't believe it," Hamilton muttered. He was like a CD player stuck on repeat. "I just can't believe it." He flopped on one of the beds and stared at the pockmarked ceiling. "He must have put a bomb in their car when he had that supercharger installed. You think?"

None of that mattered right now. The real question was, what did we do next?

"Stay in the room," I told him. "Don't make any calls."

"Where are you going?"

"Just outside. I need to think."

"You can't think in here?"

The door opened with that weird *whoomp* you get when you open a vacuum-sealed plastic container, and I stepped outside. It was the middle of the day now, and out here, a few exits down from the road to Denmark, Tennessee, the air was as fresh and clean as it got in the humid height of summer. There was a little cement picnic table under a tree on the other side of the parking lot, and I hoofed it over there to sit down.

Tall weeds bent in the breeze the trucks made as they passed on the interstate, and a butterfly danced around a beat-up old brown trash can like she was taunting it. Along the balcony on the second floor of the motel, a Hispanic lady was pushing a laundry cart and whistling a sad tune. She got drowned out when an emergency rescue vehicle screamed by, headed for the Dodge Charger and not knowing they'd be too late for anything but a marshmallow roast.

We were up the Copenhagen River without a paddle, that much was for sure. As soon as Claude found out Hamilton wasn't in that car, he'd have people out looking for him— probably even the Denmark PD. That meant whatever we did, we'd have to do it fast. I pulled out my phone. Two bars. Apparently we were close enough to civilization.

But just barely.

When I got back to the room, I brought three pizzas and drinks. Hamilton was sitting on the floor with his back against one of the beds, watching the news. He spared me a glance as I came in.

"Thought you might not come back."

"You really think that little of me?"

He shrugged. "I wouldn't have come back," he said.

"Yes, you would have." I dropped one of the pies in his lap.

"Three pizzas?" he asked.

I set the other two on the little table. "Eat," I told him.

The TV stations already had images of the smoldering Dodge Charger. This, of course, was scintillating stuff. I will never understand why people are so interested in seeing firefighters douse a burning house or watching police draw white chalk lines. Nothing like somebody else's horrible misfortune to make you feel better about your own miserable life, I guess.

"What were you doing all that time?" Hamilton asked.

"Making some calls."

I sat and started on one of the other pizzas. The news shifted back to the studio, where the story changed to an update on the girl who got sick on polluted river water. Olivia Mendelsohn was out of the hospital and expected to make a full recovery. Just in case we missed what happened, they showed her chugging the water and puking all over my feet again. I think they caught my good side. After that, they posted information on tomorrow night's emergency town hall meeting to hear more of Elsinore's excuses.

"She must really hate me," Hamilton said.

"Yeah. That's part of it."

"She's right. I deserve it."

"Aye. There's the rub."

"Will you cut it out? I'm trying to show some remorse here."

"Seriously?"

"*Yes,* seriously," he said, and he looked like he meant it. "I really screwed things up with her, and I know it. I got so mad when Mom married Claude. I felt, I don't know. Betrayed."

"And if your own mother could betray you, why not every other girl in the world?" I asked. I meant it as a joke, but when Hamilton didn't argue with me, I thought that might not actually be too far from the truth. Who needed self-help books anyway?

"I kept wanting to explain things to her. To apologize. But every time we saw each other after the breakup, I was always so angry. Or else she was."

"She had a pretty good reason, I think."

"I know. I wanted to go see her in the hospital, but I was afraid she'd throw acid on me or something."

I ate my pizza.

"You still got a thing for her, then?" I asked.

Hamilton couldn't take his eyes off the television as they showed Olivia leaving the hospital earlier today, and the look in his face was all the answer I needed. I got a lump in my throat as I swallowed a bite, and I tried to wash it down with root beer. It didn't work.

"I wish I could take it all back," he said. "Start over. Make everything up to her somehow."

"You never know," I told him, "sometimes wishes *do* come true."

He turned. "What's that supposed to mean?"

There was a knock at the door, and Hamilton freaked. I showed him my hand and went to the door to peek through the hole.

"Here," I said. I pulled a packet of envelopes from my back

pocket and tossed them on the floor beside Hamilton. He picked them up.

"Are these—are these my letters to Olivia? How did you—?"

"Just call me your fairy godmother," I told him. I pulled the door open, and there was Olivia. She looked a lot better than yesterday, which was easier without the big tube shoved down her throat. I was a heel for dragging her out here the day she got out of the hospital, but I knew she felt the same way about Hamilton as he did about her, and that deep down they still wanted to be together. She came inside, and I took her backpack and handed her the other pizza.

Olivia and Hamilton stared at each other, waiting for the other one to say something mean. Neither one did.

"Okay, kids," I said. "I'll give you a minute to make nice, and then we have to get to work."

CHAPTER TWENTY-SIX

—💀—

Judging by the parking lot in front of the Foreign Legion Hall, it looked like everybody in Denmark, Tennessee, had come to the town hall meeting. Either that or there was a pickup truck convention.

Hamilton and Olivia and I snuck inside, but the television cameras found us. Well, they found Olivia, at least. She was a featured speaker and already had a face viewers would be familiar with, although I wondered if they would recognize her when she wasn't ralphing.

That was how Claude and Mrs. Prince saw us.

"Hamilton! Oh my God!" Mrs. Prince cried, making everyone in the room shut up and watch. Dressed in all black, she sprinted down the aisle and wrapped Hamilton in an unreturned hug. "We thought you were dead!" Tears streamed down her cheeks. "Why didn't you call!? When we saw those pictures on the news, we thought—"

"That's funny," Hamilton said, "you never watch the news."

"Well, Claude had it on last night," she said, confusion crossing her brow. Maybe she was beginning to wonder about the coincidence of that. If I had to guess, I'd say Claude wasn't a regular viewer either.

Mrs. Prince hugged her son tight again. "I've been worried sick. First your father, and then you—I don't know how I would have managed."

It was the perfect setup for a cut-down, but Hamilton didn't take it. Maybe he really was sorry after all. He held her away and tried to smile.

Claude stepped up behind them. "Hamilton," he said. "How fortunate you're alive." His eyes flicked to me. "I suppose we have your friend to thank."

"All in a day's work," I told him.

Mrs. Prince hugged me too, just for old times' sake.

"I've got to get up front, Mom," Hamilton said. "I'm taking part in the debate tonight."

"What? But we've already asked Larry to represent the plant."

"I'm not arguing for the plant tonight, Mom. I'm taking the other side. Olivia's been prepping me."

The look on Mrs. Prince's face said "Huh?" The look on Claude's face said "Die."

"I've had just about enough of you and your little stunts, Hamilton. You do this, and—"

"And what, you'll send me off to another clinic? What will you do this time, cut the brakes? Or maybe you'll just send me off with some *professional* hit men."

Claude's face turned red and his neck bulged at his tight white collar. I think he might have strangled Hamilton right there if we hadn't been surrounded by a hundred witnesses.

"What's he talking about?" Mrs. Prince asked.

"See you later, Mom," said Hamilton, and we left Claude to try and cover.

Olivia was waiting by the podium. There was a lot of whispering as Hamilton took a seat on what the crowd thought was the wrong side of the table for a Prince to be on, and the camera lights turned our way. Larry the law student looked up from his briefcase and frowned. Some official—the mayor or duke or Grand Poo-bah of Denmark—quieted everybody down and promised they'd all get answers. I was hoping for the same. The floor was given to the legal counsel for Elsinore Paper International, and the duel was under way.

"Let me begin by citing recent EPA studies," Larry said, holding up some official-looking papers, "which state that Elsinore has been meeting and even exceeding pollution standards." The audience murmured their disbelief.

"Where were those studies conducted?" Hamilton interrupted. "Upstream or down?"

"Random locations, per government regulations," Larry explained. "The exact location of each test doesn't matter. When taken together—"

Hamilton held up a Styrofoam cup of coffee and a glass of water.

"Doesn't matter? This is clean," he said, lifting the water. "And this coffee is dirty. You test the water, you pass. You test the coffee, you fail. You average those out . . ." Hamilton poured coffee into the glass of water, where it turned a semi-clear, tan color. "You average those out, and you get something else that just barely passes. But what about this part?" he asked. He tipped the cup toward the audience so they could see the coffee inside. "Does that look clean to you?" The crowd broke into applause, and suddenly Hamilton went from villain to champion.

Larry straightened his tie. "Elsinore Paper has met or

exceeded government mandated testing and standards," he repeated, drawing boos from the audience.

"What do you mean exceeded?" Hamilton asked.

"I mean that Elsinore has actually conducted more tests than is required by law. The EPA requests testing twice a year. Claude Prince took samples more than a dozen times the past six months alone."

I made a point of finding Claude in the crowd. He was sitting right down front, and he looked like he had swallowed a gallon of the Copenhagen River. His eyes met mine, and I gave him my best imitation of his own crap-eating smile and goofy wave.

"My uncle took dozens of samples? He was the Elsinore chemist in charge of pollution testing?"

"Yes," Larry said, glad for the chance to prove his argument. "His signature is on every one of these documents."

Claude was glancing around, no doubt already plotting his escape route. I hoped one of the camera crews was getting his reactions. I wanted to buy a copy of the tape and watch it when I needed a good laugh.

"So Claude Prince had the means at his disposal to test for dioxin—to separate that chemical compound out in the Elsinore lab."

"Well—yes. But I don't see where you're going with this."

That was my cue. I stepped up to the podium and spread the medical records for Hamilton's father out in front of me.

"Each one of us has about five to ten parts per trillion of dioxin in our bodies," I explained. "A week before Rex Prince died, his doctor found *two thousand* times that amount in his body." I turned to Larry. "Now, who did you say was testing for all that dioxin?"

The town hall meeting about pollution had suddenly

become an impromptu murder trial, and the audience was pretty quick to keep up. Scandalized murmurs ripped through the crowd as the smart ones explained it to the dumb ones: Claude Prince had poisoned his brother with dioxin samples taken from the river. In the front row, Trudy Prince stood. She must have felt poisoned herself, in a way. I noticed Claude didn't rush to her side this time. He was rushing somewhere else.

The camera lights found Claude already up from his chair and moving toward the exit. That's where Miranda got him. My sister with the Knoxville Police Department. She had been one of my calls yesterday, and she had driven all night to be here today. She was cool like that. I was pleased to see she had brought a couple of state troopers with her too.

"Trudy," Claude pleaded. "It's not true. You have to believe me. This is just some wild story!"

"This might help," I said, signaling Olivia. She handed me the coffee tin out of her backpack, and I pulled out the videotape from the security camera. "This is a video of Hamilton's father telling us he'd been poisoned. And this," I said, pulling out a bottle sealed in an oversized plastic bag, "this is the bottle of Johnnie Walker Black Label that Rex Prince had been drinking from the Friday night before he died. My guess is it's loaded with dioxin, just like the ones he drank for the last few months of his life."

Motive, means, opportunity. I had it all.

"That's not true!" Claude protested. "I'm being framed!"

"What, because you think you got rid of the real bottle?" I asked him. "That bottle you took from the cabinet Saturday afternoon was brand-new. I just poured half of it out to make it look like this one. I had already snagged the original one— making sure not to smear any fingerprints."

The town hall meeting turned into total bedlam then, and the camera crews split between covering Claude's arrest and interviewing me, Hamilton, and Olivia.

"I'm just happy to finally bring my father's killer to justice," Hamilton told a reporter. "And now that real evidence of Elsinore's environmental abuse has come to light, I pledge as a future owner to do whatever it takes to clean up the Copenhagen River. With the dedicated help of community activists like Olivia Mendelsohn, of course."

Olivia took him and kissed him then, nice and hard, and the cameras got it all. They were back together—maybe for good—and that was a tape I *wouldn't* be asking the networks for. I went to catch up with my sister. On the way, I ran into Ford N. Branff and Candy the Cowboy leaving together.

"It appears that Hamilton has had a change of heart," Branff told me.

"Yeah, I guess he wants the place after all. Sorry."

He sighed. "Well, there are always other companies to conquer."

Candy gave me a little salute with his chin as they left. *"Ciao, pescado."*

Miranda was just finishing with one of the troopers when I walked up to give her the bottle and the tape.

"Damn, Horatio. You sure do like to stir the pot."

"You think it'll be enough?" I asked. Miranda shrugged.

"For attempted murder, maybe. It'll be awfully hard to pin him on 'death by cancer.'"

"Attempted murder isn't enough, but it'll do."

"I'll be sure to tell the judge you're okay with that, then," she said, mocking me. "Oh, and you'll be interested to know the two vics in the burning car died from a jury-rigged regulator, set to detonate when the car topped one hundred. Same kind of thing they use in trucks to keep them from accelerating past a certain speed."

I nodded. "Claude was the mechanic for Elsinore Paper once. He'd know how to do that."

Miranda shook her head. "Remind me to call you in the next time I find a body."

"I'm a hundred dollars a day, plus expenses," I told her. I glanced across the room at Hamilton and Olivia with their arms around each other, still talking to cameras. "Unless you're a friend. Then it's all part of the service."

"You know, there's this girl who lives down the hall from me," Miranda told me. "Has a nose ring and wears clothes a size too small, but I think you'd like her—"

"Hold that thought," I told her. "Forever."

Across the room, Hamilton was having a heart-to-heart with his mother, and Olivia was just finishing a chat with Larry. I weaved my way over before someone stuck another microphone in her face.

"Hey," she said.

"Hey yourself."

"So. You did it. Somehow you busted Claude and got Elsinore to clean up its act and got me and Hamilton back together all at the same time. You're pretty amazing, you know that?"

"It's the popular theory," I told her.

"You know, you'd almost be cute if you weren't so damn full of yourself."

"I thought that's what put me over the top."

We stood there for a moment, just a tiny fraction of a nanosecond in the history of the ever-shifting, ever-changing cosmos, staring straight into each other's eyes.

"So, anything I can do to thank you?" she asked.

"Well, there is *one* thing . . ." I said.

Olivia narrowed her eyes and smiled. She stood on her toes to kiss me, and I let her. It was everything I thought it would be, times ten.

"Thanks," I said when we were finished. "But I meant my hat."

Olivia pulled my Cardinals hat off and stuck it in my hands.

"Thanks for the loaner," she said.

Hamilton came back and put his arm around her. If he had seen us kiss he wasn't making a thing out of it, which I figured was fair, considering we'd both taken crap from him for weeks.

"He trying to tell you this was all his doing?"

"Wasn't it?" Olivia asked.

Hamilton grinned and clapped a hand on my shoulder. "He just doesn't want to admit that I was right about Claude from the start."

"Maybe. But you were wrong about one thing," I told him, pulling my cap down tight. "You never do get used to the smell."

TURN THE PAGE FOR A PREVIEW OF:

something

A Horatio Wilkes Mystery

wicked

CHAPTER ONE

— 1 —

History is full of guys who did stupid things for women. Paris started the Trojan War over Helen. Mark Antony abandoned Rome for Cleopatra. John Lennon gave up the Beatles for Yoko Ono. You can say I'm a dreamer, but they're not the only ones. Like my friend Joe Mackenzie: He was about to jump off a five-story building just to impress a girl.

"Come on, you wuss!" Mac's girlfriend Beth yelled. "If you don't jump off that tower, you're not getting any more of this!" She lifted her sweater up over her head, showing her bra and her extraordinary breasts to Mac, me, Banks, and the five or six other people milling around Kangaroo Kevin's Bungee Jump-O-Rama in Pigeon Forge, Tennessee. They actually inspired a small round of applause. I won't say what they did to me, but Beth's fun cushions certainly inspired Mac. With a Scottish war cry he charged the end of the platform and jumped headfirst, screaming all the way down. His kilt opened like a daisy as he fell, and everyone saw his stamen.

"Wooooohooooo!" Beth called.

"Oh, for the love of Dirk Diggler," I muttered. "Only Mac would go bungee jumping in a kilt without any underwear on." I chose to look at Beth instead. She had covered herself back up, but the image of those perfect breasts was burned into my retinas, like when you look into a lightbulb too long and all you see for the next five minutes is the blinding afterglow of the filament.

"Get a good look, Horatio?" Beth asked.

"Of *Mac*, yes. If you could do that sweater thing again, though, I would very much appreciate it."

Bashful Banks looked away in case Beth took me up on it, which wasn't likely. Behind us, Mac's screams turned to laughter as he and all his dangling parts bounded into the air on the bungee cord. Beth proved she could multitask, watching Mac bounce and giving me the finger at the same time.

"Not even if every other boy in the world was covered from head to toe in zits and back hair," she told me.

Beth *was* out of my league. She was so far out of my league, in fact, that she was the New York Yankees and I was the Weehawken five- and six-year-old tee-ball B team. She was built like the top half of a lingerie model grafted onto the bottom half of a ballet dancer. She was also a freshman in college, and she suffered us high school juniors like a goddess among the muck-farmers. Beth's dad and Mac's dad were business partners, which was how they'd met, but beyond his male model good looks I'd never understood why she dated beneath herself.

Mac bungeed to a stop, and Beth ran to give him his earthly reward.

"Man, would you ever do that?" Banks asked.

"Not even for those marvelous Dolly Partons," I told him. "That boy is seriously whipped."

Banks sighed, and I wondered if he wasn't thinking right now that he'd be happy to be whipped if it meant having a girlfriend. Don't get me wrong—Wallace Banks was a great guy. He was also some distant relative of Mac's, which automatically let him run around with the king and queen of the Highland Games. But no amount of being nice or being Mac's second cousin once removed or whatever could ever really overcome wearing a white button-down short-sleeve shirt with a pen-filled pocket protector. He was also wearing a red tartan kilt and matching pom-pom beret, and just below his pasty knees he had on white woolen hose held up with ribbons. That we were in town to attend the Mount Birnam Scottish Highland Games made the getup somewhat excusable; that Banks wore this outfit on a daily basis made him a total geek—but a lovable one.

Mac came wobbling up with Beth wrapped around him. She was breathing harder than he was.

"I can't feel my legs!" he said.

"I think you've lost feeling in your brain too," I told him.

"There is a *cushion*," Mac said. We'd had this argument twenty minutes ago. "It was completely safe. They wouldn't let you do it if you could get hurt!"

"Mac, you signed a waiver that said you wouldn't sue them if you *died*. Does that sound completely safe to you? And a four-foot-tall inflatable bag wasn't going to do a whole lot of good if that cord snapped."

"You're just jealous, Horatio. You've got to try it! Woo! What a rush!"

Mac's knees went out from under him and Beth couldn't hold him up. I caught him, and Banks and I steered him toward a bench while Beth bounced away to buy him a bottle of water.

"The next time you go bungee jumping in a kilt, wear some underwear, will you?" I told him.

Mac grinned. "A real Scot wears naught beneath his kilt but a draught, Horatio."

"You're not a real Scot. You were born in Chattanooga."

"I'm Scott*ish*. Besides," Mac said, flicking the end of Banks's kilt, "Beth likes me freeballing. Better access, you know?"

I held up my hands. "Too much information."

Where Banks's kilt was a fashion disaster, Mac managed to look studly in his skirt. It was blue and red and he wore it with a T-shirt that had the blue and white Scottish flag with the words "X Marks the Scot" underneath. And Mac would have eaten haggis before wearing the dorky white socks and ribbons Banks wore; instead he showed off his tan, muscular legs in nothing more than a worn pair of hiking boots. But for a short mop of brown hair instead of long flowing locks he could have doubled for one of those beefcakes on the covers of romance novels.

"Your dagger's showing," I told him.

Mac frowned and adjusted himself under his kilt.

"Not your metaphorical dagger, Spartacus. Your literal one." I pointed at his shoe. The little dagger he wore in his sock had come loose during the bungee jump. It was a Scottish thing; Banks had one tucked into his sock too.

"Your *sgian dubh*," Banks told him.

"Yeah. What he said."

Mac stuck the thing back in his sock. "Oh man, was Beth all *over* me when they unstrapped me. Just wait 'til tonight at the campground."

"Mac, you're always letting her make you do stupid things," I said.

"She's not making me do anything I don't already want to do."

"He's hooked on Beth Amphetamine," Banks said.

"Yeah. You need to kick the habit."

Beth came prancing up with a bottle of water. "What I need is a little more Beth," Mac said for her benefit. And his. She sat on his lap with a twirl of her skirt.

Of the four of us, I was the only one wearing pants.

"Gee," I said, "maybe someday I'll have a girlfriend who makes me jump off buildings too."

Beth played with Mac's hair. "One of those people who follows you around is talking again, Mac. Make him go away, will you?"

Mac lifted Beth off his lap and he stood, ignoring our sniping like always. "We've only got an hour before we need to be up the mountain. What else do we want to do?"

"There's a Tartan Museum we could go see," said Banks.

Beth looked at him like he had just grown a third eyeball.

"We could maybe set fire to the Gooder than Grits restaurant and hope it spreads to the rest of this tourist trap hell," I offered.

Beth started hopping up and down. "I want to go back to that fortune-teller's! The one we passed. What was it called?"

"Madame Hecate's?" I said.

"I want Mac to have his palm read!" Beth sang.

"Here, hold it out and I'll slap it," I told him. He held out his hands and I tried to smack them and make them red, but he pulled away in time.

"I don't want to go to some stupid psychic," Mac said. "Let's go get funnel cakes."

Beth pressed her boobs into Mac. "But I *want* you to have your fortune read, Mac."

"Okay, okay. We can come down the mountain and hit the Tartan Museum later," he told Banks. "And maybe we'll have time for a funnel cake before we go back. Right now we'll do Madame Hoodoo or whatever."

Beth took Mac by the arm and pulled him away.

"Meow," Banks said.

I made a sound like a whip cracking and we followed along down the strip.

Pigeon Forge sits like a scar in the earth, a gaping, brightly colored wound festering in the Smoky Mountain sun. It's not a town; it's an eight-lane abomination of go-cart tracks, mini-golf courses, and comedy barns, peopled with Elvis impersonators and neon orange fiberglass gorillas. The dappled green mountains in the background occasionally threaten to reclaim Pigeon Forge and engulf it like kudzu, but at the last minute some new developer will add another outlet mall or country music theater or pancake house and beat back the horrible darkness.

We found Madame Hecate's Psychic Readings wedged in between a funnel cake stall and an airbrush T-shirt hut. A sign in the window said: "Palms Read While You Wait."

Mac pushed his way inside and a bell tinkled, I suppose so Madame Hecate wouldn't have to waste any of her considerable psychic talents on predicting our arrival. The little room was decorated in a combination of Late Victorian and Pier 1. The walls were covered with old black-and-white portraits in gilded frames, and funky beaded lampshades draped with red handkerchiefs did what little they could to give the place some atmosphere. A plug-in fountain spewing clouds of dry ice bubbled in the corner, and in the center of the room stood a small table where it looked like someone had been playing solitaire with tarot cards.

"Excellent!" said Beth.

Something brushed my leg and I nearly jumped.

"That is Graymalkin, my, how you say? Familiar," said a voice.

The gray cat certainly was getting familiar with my black Converse. Meanwhile Madame Hecate, the source of the creepy accent, ran a hand up the wooden door frame on the other side of the room. I think she was trying to be mysterious. The fortune-teller was round like a crystal ball, and had her black hair tied back in a yellow bandana. She wore a long flowing gown that *shushed* as she shifted, and in the strange light I could see she had whiskers on her chin. It wasn't so much disgusting as embarrassing: Madame Hecate could grow a better beard than I could.

She slid her hand back down the door frame, then suddenly jerked it away.

"Ach!"

"What's wrong?" Beth asked.

The woman sucked a finger. "It is nothing. A splinter. I prick my thumb."

"Too bad she didn't see that coming," I muttered.

"Who comes to see Madame Hecate?"

At her invitation we sat in folding chairs around the table, and Mac gave her our names.

"*Horatio* your name is?" she said after I'd been introduced.

"Seriously," I told her, "you of all people do not want to go there."

"I want you to read Mac's palm," Beth told her.

"Is twenty dollars for full reading," said Madame Hecate. I snorted, but Beth already had a twenty out on the table. I shook my head. P. T. Barnum was still right.

In the only real magic she was going to perform that day, Madame Hecate palmed the twenty and made it disappear. Then she took Mac's hand in her own and began tracing the lines on his palm.

"Ah, yes, your fate line is strong," she said. "Very strong. But here—the heart and head line are fused. You think and act at same time, yes?"

"That's true!" said Beth. "He's very impulsive."

"Ah," she said. "And I see you are here for . . . some kind of festival. A competition."

"Well, kind of, yeah," Mac said.

"The . . . Highland Games?" she asked.

"What gave it away," I asked, "the kilts or the funny hat?"

"Hey," Banks said.

"A festival, yes, but you are not competing?"

"I didn't make the clan team," Mac confessed.

I had to admit, the woman's act was good. She certainly had Mac, Beth, and Banks snowed. They watched her work Mac's palm like she was revealing the hidden secrets of the universe.

"But make the team you will," she told him. "And not only will you compete, you will win!"

"You mean the Highland decathlon? I win it?"

"You're not even in it," I reminded him. To Hecate I said, "He missed the cut."

"For you, fate is sealed. You will compete, and you will win," Hecate said, ignoring me again. "And you will be king of the mountain!"

Beth gasped in delight and hugged Mac around his shoulders.

Mac nodded, happy with his fate. "King of the mountain. I could get used to that."

"What about me?" asked Banks. He reached into his sporran—a traditional Scottish waist pouch that was the ancestor of the fanny pack—and pulled out another twenty.

"Oh, not you too," I said.

Banks blushed and shrugged, but he still handed over an Andy Jackson.

Madame Hecate took his palm and gave it the same treatment.

"You, your life line is strong, but you are not athlete," she said. I huffed at her mastery of the obvious, but apparently no one was listening to me now. "For you, there is other competition? Music, perhaps?"

Oh, she was good all right. That had been a complete guess, but it was spot on.

"The bagpipes," Banks offered. "I play the bagpipes. There's this really important tournament, and the winner gets—"

"You are lesser than your friend, but greater," Madame Hecate told him. "I see you not so happy, yet much happier."

Banks frowned. "I don't—"

"While that one will be king of mountain, it is you who will *own* mountain."

"Me?" Banks asked. "Own Mount Birnam you mean?"

For all the laughing they'd done about coming here, Mac and Banks were deadly serious now. Beth crossed her arms and frowned.

"Is all I see." She turned to me. "I read your fortune, Horatio?"

I loaded up a short laugh with derision and disbelief and let her have it.

"Right," I said. "Let me guess. You see a crease bisecting my life line, which means I'll soon have some kind of big test or trial. And when I get to this great, vague, unnamed challenge, I should just listen to my heart, right?"

She took my palm in her hand and I rolled my eyes. I got a cold shiver, though, like the temperature in the room had just dropped ten degrees. I tried not to let anybody see me shake.

"Heart line is strong, yes, but head line is stronger. You think, think, think, which is good," she told me. "But this time you will listen *too much* to heart. It is head you must learn to hear again."

She was right about me thinking too much. I almost started to believe she had some kind of power, then shook it off. *Of course* she knew I used my head more than my heart—I'd been the only one playing the skeptic. As for the cold shiver, she'd probably turned up the air-conditioning when she heard us come in.

"I hope you're not expecting to get paid for that one," I told her.

"No. That one is free," she told me. "But you will be back. Then you will pay me."

"Right," I said. "Don't bet on it."

We sat through Beth's fortune—something vague about having gall for milk and a snake under a flower—and the mystic rose from the table. "Madame Hecate is tired now. Must, how you say? Recharge batteries."

"Wait, how do you know I'll—" Mac started to ask, but Madame Hecate disappeared into the next room.

"Happy now?" I asked them. "Sixty bucks for five minutes of flimflam. The next time you jokers want somebody to blow hot air up your kilts, let me know. I'll be happy to take your money."

Nobody was listening. Mac and Banks had fortune and glory in their eyes, and Beth was no doubt lost in some fantasy where she was wearing a tiara. We filed back outside and made for Mac's SUV. For a time, everyone was lost in their own daydreams.

Mac gave Banks a punch in the arm. "Hey cousin, you're going to own the mountain!"

It woke Banks up and he smiled. "And you're going to be king of the games!"

"And I'm going to be queen," Beth said.

"Right," I said. "Which is all just about as likely as me wearing a kilt."

They chuckled, but I could tell they didn't think it was funny. As we climbed into the car for the trip up the mountain, I saw Beth squeeze Mac's hand and pull him down to whisper in his ear.

If I'd been paying attention then, really listening with my head and not my heart, I might have heard it. It was the whisper of something coming.

Something wicked.